Bliss

by

Gini Rifkin

Fae Warriors, Book 2

Bliss

COPYRIGHT © 2016 by Gini Rifkin

Cover Art by *Debbie Taylor*

The Wild Rose Press, Inc.
PO Box 708
Adams Basin, NY 14410-0708
Visit us at www.thewildrosepress.com

Publishing History
First Fantasy Rose Edition, 2016
Print ISBN 978-1-5092-1112-8
Digital ISBN 978-1-5092-1113-5

Fae Warriors, Book 2
Published in the United States of America

Bliss eased up out of her chair.

Nate stood transfixed as she began to morph into warrior mode.

Like liquid silver, the bracelets she wore transformed into armor protection for her hands and forearms. She grew taller, leaner, meaner, her eyes flashing. When her wings materialized he took a step back. They were gleaming metal, appearing deceptively fragile, but the talons along the edges appeared sharp and deadly—dispelling any doubt the wings were made for battle. Giving a few preemptive flaps, she sent up a wave of dust, reminding him of an armed-to-the-teeth Victoria's Secret model. But now was hardly the time for waxing poetic.

Jamming his Stetson on more securely, he retrieved his lariat, grabbed the reins, and leapt onto the mare's back. Riding without a saddle wouldn't have been his first choice, but being the only choice, it'd have to do.

"Easy girl," he murmured, when the mare danced to one side. The little dun, one of his best, would be facing a predator worse than the mountain lion they'd come upon last year. He could only hope she'd muster the same passel of courage today as she did then.

With an ungodly roar, the two Reps charged out of the woods. Their gruesome reality surpassed all the pictures he'd concocted in his mind. The mare snorted, but stood fast. With a war cry making his hair stand on end, Bliss shot straight up into the air.

Praise for Gini Rifkin

"The characters [in *SOLACE: FAE WARRIORS BOOK 1*] are well-written and the plot is seamless. I look forward to reading book two."

~*Between the Pages (4 Stars)*
~*~

"[*A COWBOY'S FATE* is a] must read."

~*Still Moments Magazine (5 Stars)*
~*~

"[*VICTORIAN DREAM* is] written with a rich depth of detail."

~*Night Owl Reviews*

~*~

"The chemistry between these two excellent characters [in *SPECIAL DELIVERY*] is riveting."

~*Still Moments Magazine (5 Stars; a Publisher's Pick)*
~*~

"*IRON HEART* gives the classic epic adventures a run for their money."

~*Sizzling Hot Books (5 Hearts)*
~*~

"I highly recommend [*LADY GALLANT*] to any fan of historical romance."

~*Long and Short Reviews*
~*~

"[*THE DRAGON AND THE ROSE*] is an *enchanting* story!"

~*Long and Short Reviews*

Dedication

Dedicated to Norma and Carol.
Two amazing women who
truly embody the spirit of the West.
Day or night, ready to lend a hand, no questions asked.
You've taught me so much
about caring for my animals,
and about getting on with life.
I'm so fortunate to call you my friends,
and so proud you call me yours.

~*~

With thanks and gratitude to The Wild Rose Press,
and my wonderful editor, Amanda Barnett.

Author's Note:

Fae Warriors' glossary of terms is found after page 236.

During the Great War, Earthlings known as Milesian defeated the Fae, sentencing them to live underground. Saddened because Man had turned his back on them, the Faerie-folk grew smaller, destined to thrive in hills and burrows—all but one clan. They languished in the darkness, on the verge of extinction. Spirited away to another galaxy by Mother Nature, the tribe survived, growing larger and stronger, their code of honor unshakable, and their devotion to Mother unwavering.

They are the Fae Warriors, Guardians of the Multiverse.

Three such warriors are the Sisters of Anu.

~*~

Chapter One

Present day: Boulder, Colorado, autumn

Noodge, her beloved Rapran, yanked against his collar nearly jerking the leash from Bliss' hand. He was on the hunt—for something big. Bliss scoped out the dog park, her Fae senses not detecting anything amiss. Nearly an hour until sunrise, there were no humans to be seen. Even the squirrels appeared to still be sleeping.

She enjoyed the predawn quiet, the only time she could walk the creature without causing a ruckus, or running into the Animal Control lady. The unrelenting woman patrolled the area as if it was a prison exercise yard, and so far they'd already had two narrow escapes.

"Slow down, Noodge," she ordered, but the command seemed to fall on big, furry, deaf ears.

Her Fae Warrior sisters, Solace and Portence loved Noodge too, but only Bliss had a modicum of control over him. And she had to admit, the otherworldly creature could be a handful. In a vain attempt to make the Rapacious Ranivorous appear more domesticated, they'd trimmed his hair and dyed some of his yellowish stripes to a more harmonious hue. Still, the Rapran resembled a spectacular combination of Tibetan mastiff, Bengal tiger, and Black-tailed wallaby.

Hanging on for dear life, Bliss flash-moved behind Noodge when he rocketed out of the park and down the street. Even using this fast-forward mode of transport, perfect for covering ground quickly, she could barely keep pace with him. They ended up in a blind alley, towering walls of weathered brick surrounded them on three sides. To the right stood the backdoors to a beauty parlor and a shoe repair shop. On the left, the kitchen exit of a combo restaurant/lounge.

Noodge snuffled the ground, his growly-whine indicating there were Reptiles in the vicinity, or at least one had passed by recently.

What were the Reptiles up to these days? Thank the stars the wave of dead prostitutes had ended after Solace and her human partner, Captain Tanner Jackson, had eliminated Mr. Smith—a reptile posing as a Hume or human. The Priselet Corporation he'd run had quickly gone out of business too, and good riddance to them both. But what about his frenemy, Jones? To all appearances, the Rep had gone to ground with the others, but somehow she didn't buy that probable scenario.

Bliss' furry baby braced his front paws up against the building on the left, a growl rumbling in his chest as he sniffed the air.

"Hush, Noodge, be easy," she ordered. "I'll take a look-see, but you mustn't give us away."

This time the big bundle of heart and hair obediently sat down, head cocked, ears on alert.

Slipping free of her coat, Bliss materialized a small set of utility wings—another blouse ruined as they tore through the cotton material. She needed to speak to Mother Nature about upping her clothing allowance.

Gaining altitude, she flattened the front of her body against the wall, the bricks still cool from the night air.

Edging sideways, she peeked in the high window. The glass, clouded with years of accumulated dirt, revealed little, just a dimly lit room, an ordinary office. However, things got more interesting when a man entered. Too bad the hat he wore obscured his face.

He flipped on a wall switch, flooding the room with light. She drew back, but continued to watch. Crossing over to the tall stand-alone safe, wedged into one corner, he keyed in the combination, shoved the lever downward, and with obvious effort swung open the reinforced metal door. Crammed full of money from top to bottom, the safe appeared so tightly packed she doubted a handful of faerie dust would fit inside.

Liberating a small bundle of bills, he ruffled the edges and sniffed at it as if it were a fine wine. Pinot Dinero. Leaving the safe wide-open, he ambled toward the desk, cradling the money in his arm. Halfway there, he took off his hat and tossed it Frisbee-style onto a chair.

He wore a smug smile on his lips, and a set of nasty scars on his neck and left cheek. The disfigurement appeared to be from burns, the marks running upwards onto his scalp leaving his hair short, spotty, and unattractive. She jerked away in surprise, smacking her left knee against the brick wall. Scars or no scars, she recognized the scaly wretch. It was the repugnant Mr. Jones, in his somewhat worse for wear human form.

She'd been right, he hadn't left town, and apparently he'd already reinvented himself in a new entrepreneurial capacity. It hadn't taken him long to heal after his encounter with her sister, Solace, and the drone. But then reptiles were like that. They could even regrow appendages, other than their heads. Apparently they weren't as good at re-growing hair.

Hovering beside the window, she stared down at Noodge. Tongue lolling, tail wagging, he pranced back and forth from one front paw to the other. He seemed totally innocent, but when so ordered, his playful attitude could turn to death-dealing aggression. *Good boy. You earned your keep today,* she mentally praised, longing to add a tummy rub and a pat on the head. His tracking down Jones should squash any doubts about keeping the big unruly animal around.

Her body twitched with the urge to morph into warrior mode, but she held off. What if there were other Reps in the building? Things could get messy. Options flickered through her mind. Noodge hadn't been in training long enough to send him off alone for help. To be honest, even leaving him here in stakeout mode would be extremely chancy.

She closed her eyes, summoning her sisters. No luck. Eyes open, she glanced around. The canyon-like walls of solid brick were blocking her connection. If she gained elevation higher than the rooftops, maybe—

"There you are, you mangy interloper." Tranq gun strapped to her hip, the Animal Control woman hustled down the alleyway waving her ticket book like a battle flag. "I thought I saw you in the park. And no tags on your collar. You won't get away this time."

Holy Hector, they'd been had. Noodge roared, the hair-raising sound ending in a bloodcurdling howl. The hullabaloo gave the woman pause. Apparently, it also garnered Jones' attention. The window beside her creaked open. Bliss shot straight up to the roof, hunkered down, and peered over the gutter.

"What's going on down there," Jones groused, hanging out the window far enough for her to see the top of his mutilated head.

"Don't worry mister," the woman called up to him. "I got this handled." Having an audience seemed to spur the stalwart but foolish woman into action, and she went for the tranq gun.

Noodge mustn't be hurt or captured, although the dose the woman carried would most likely only irritate the huge critter. Regardless, it would lead to chaos. The woman had picked the wrong pooch to pinch.

Standing tall, she cloaked her image. To obfuscate or becloud, didn't actually turn her invisible, but using the laws of modality governed by an enchantment known only to the Fae it simply rendered her unseen— there really was a difference.

Launching herself off the roof, Bliss executed a downward fly-by maneuver, knocking the tranq gun out of the woman's hand. Then she hovered and waited, sending a mental command for Noodge to stay in position.

The woman spun around, looking first one way and then the other, anger and confusion contorting her features. Bliss glanced up at the window. Jones had disappeared. The Reps were familiar with Raprans. Had he recognized Noodge as being one? They needed to get out of here pronto.

As she telepathically told Noodge to come, the overzealous woman grabbed a broken mop handle from a nearby dumpster and took a swing at him. Flying rats. This broad was crazy. The Rapran easily scrambled out of the way then turned and waited. The woman had more balls than brains, in this case a possibly lethal combination.

Bliss caught the woman from behind and shoved her across the alley, but before she could abscond with Noodge, a movement up the passageway caught her attention. Big trouble headed their way. Raprans couldn't fly, and with their enemy blocking the only path to the street, there would be no avoiding a fight. Yet, a frisson of excitement speared through her as she hovered, still unseen.

The sky, now blushed with the soft light of dawn, shed an ironic rosy glow on the brawny figure in human form striding their way. Tall, and sporting a full head of hair, it couldn't be Jones. It must be one of his henchmen. With each unhurried step, the image blurred then reconfigured, morphing quickly into reptile. The face elongated to accommodate a set of pointy teeth— teeth dripping with saliva as if anticipating the taste of flesh. Fingernails turned to claws, and a tail appeared, as lethal a weapon as any handheld firearm. Clothes rendered too small, fell away in shreds revealing a muscular body covered with scales, and the thick haloing of hair dissolved into dust, leaving a smooth head with a ridge of sharp vestigial quills running down the long slender neck.

Bliss dropped her cover and landed near Noodge. Upgrading to metal-tipped battle wings, she drew her particle laser and took aim. The Animal Control woman groaned, and started to get up.

"Stay down," Bliss ordered.

The disagreeable woman didn't listen, or hadn't heard. Clamoring to her feet she staggered forward, blocking a clear shot at their approaching enemy.

The Rep, in all its hideous glory, kept coming—

closing in fast. Not missing a step, he backhanded the obstinate woman out of the way, sending her crashing against the bricks and mortar. A bloody streak marked the wall behind her as her limp body slid to the ground.

Halting abruptly, the lizard-brain turned and whipped his tail around, scraping up a cloud of dust and trash. Noodge jumped over the deadly appendage then leaped on the attacker's back like a lion on a gazelle. A horrid deadly gazelle, not ready to give up the fight.

Again Bliss held her fire, this time not willing to risk hitting Noodge. Crouched and at the ready, she tried not to worry. This was what Raprans were trained for, and they'd learned their lessons well. After Mother Nature had rescued them from torment, she'd bred the hurt and uncontrollable aggression from them so they could serve the good side, so they could stand with the Fae Warrior Alpha Team.

The Rapran's claws ripped into the Rep's shoulders. Green blood spurted, and a putrid smell overshadowed the other back-alley odors. When Noodge sank his teeth in deep and ripped out the Rep's throat, it was all over but the shouting. Head nearly decapitated, her enemy would bleed out soon, but Bliss had no intention of waiting. They had to get out of here before a crowd gathered, or the police showed up.

"Stand down, boy," she ordered.

Out of protocol rather than mercy, she laser blasted the Rep's head from his body, putting him out of his misery while insuring he would never recover. Flash moving over to the Animal Control woman, she checked for a pulse, but found none. As irritating and uncompromising as the woman had been, she hadn't deserve such an ending. No one did.

Wings dematerialized, Bliss and Noodge ran for home.

****

"The safe is as empty as this room. Are you sure it was him," Port asked, for what seemed like the hundredth time.

"Do the Manshees of Ceti 9 have both boobs and balls? Of course I'm sure," Bliss said with a huff, wishing to tie Port's long white hair in a knot—around her neck.

Except for hair color, weapon choice, and the kind of men they sought, Bliss and her two sisters, Port and Solace were identical triplets. Port the eldest, by a mere few minutes, could get bossy on occasion, and Bliss usually let it slide. After all, regardless of the pecking order, they each had their good and bad points. Today however, Bliss wasn't in the mood for her sister's dominating air.

By the time they had returned to the scene with the U.S. Army ET Squad, Mr. Jones and the money were gone. Capturing Jones and confiscating the funds used for bankrolling the Reps, would have been a real plus.

"It was *him*," Bliss said adamantly, unable to curb the irritation in her voice. Being the youngest, she sometimes went overboard with the need to prove herself.

Crossing the room to where Jones had stood, she glanced out the open window. You could still see green blood where the unknown Fae Eater had gone down, and red where the Hume had died. One good death, one bad. The fact that Reptiles were on Earth remained classified information, so Tanner's ET squad had been called in to perform the odious and odorous task of cleaning up what remained of the Rep. Then and only then had the local police and the ME had been allowed into the alley to take care of the Animal Control woman.

Fists clenched at her side Bliss turned back around. The Fae Warriors had been ordered here to save the Earth and protect civilians. Today she hadn't accomplished her mission.

Port settled a comforting arm across Bliss' shoulders. "Don't get your red hair in a twist. It wasn't your fault he got away."

"If not mine, whose? And I feel badly we had a human casualty. Wrong place at the wrong time isn't going to be much comfort to her family."

Solace spun around to face them. "Bliss, don't you dare take on such an unreasonable burden of responsibility. You contained the situation as best you could," she insisted. "As best as anyone could."

"Noodge held his own, that's for sure," Bliss added, focusing on the big bundle of crazy she loved so much. "He showed no fear battling that nasty Rep."

"Even I agree having Noodge along turned out to be a good thing," Port relented. "If it wasn't for the big hairball, we wouldn't have known Jones and his boys were still holed up in this area."

"There's sure plenty of DNA and prints in this office." Solace flipped her long black braid out of the way as she bent down to collect a green Reptile scale. "Guess they didn't have time to scrub it down, or didn't care. Either way, we'll verify Jones lived here, and maybe get a handle on the identity of his followers."

"Best of all," Captain Jackson praised, as he sauntered into the room, "there's one less Rep on the loose, which counts for a lot." Crossing over he stood beside Solace. "We're out of here, babe," he informed her with a peck on the cheek, and a lingering pat to her backside. "My men reconnoitered the entire perimeter and haven't found any evidence as to where he's gone. We'll widen the search on the way back to HQ, but don't hold your breath."

The good Captain and her sister were much more than combat partners. And who could blame Solace. An ex-Army Ranger, and all alpha-male, Tanner headed up the Army E.T. Squad. He took his job and her sister seriously, and he filled out his black T-shirt and camo pants like a superhero—and Bliss should know, defenders of justice and graphic novels were her addiction.

"So what's on your training docket for the rest of the day?" Solace asked him.

"More water rescue maneuvers. The river is different every day, so the training has to be too."

"Okay. Stay safe. And thanks for letting me know. I'll catch up with you later."

Solace gave Tanner a deep kiss goodbye, and watched him leave.

"I just can't get enough of my Hume," she sighed.

Port, of course, still refused to even look sideways at a Hume, but Bliss had high hopes for her new partner. Not necessarily in the lover department, although she couldn't discount the heady attraction she felt for him. Behind those horn-rimmed glasses Nathaniel Winston Calhoun had possibilities. She'd recognized an especially good aura when she saw one.

"I'm out of here, too," Bliss said. "Don't want to be late to finally see the blasted clock, or I should say clocks?" Her human partner worked at the Boulder site which housed the cesium fountain atomic clock, timekeeper of the world.

"Don't tell me there's more than one now," Port said, surprise evident in her voice.

"I'll say. There's two of them, I guess that's why all the delay in me taking a tour. Until today, they were still setting up the NIST-F2. It's called the Ytterbium Atomic Clock, and it's about 10 billion times more precise than your basic quartz timepiece."

"You're kidding." Solace closed the last forensic bag, and tucked it into her field kit with the others.

"There's no kidding around when you talk to these guys about their precious clocks. When I stopped there before, and couldn't wrangle a tour, I casually joked *'well that's okay. I'll just wait until it comes out in wristwatch size'* they looked at me like they'd already been informed I came from another planet."

"Are you worried about seeing Dr. Calhoun now that he knows you're Fae?"

"I have to admit I am. I wanted to breach the subject in person, after he had a chance to form an opinion based on who I am regardless of what I am."

"I'm sorry things didn't work out the way you wanted, Bliss," Port said. "And doubly glad I'll never have to worry about such a conundrum. If I ever get to meet my new partner, it won't matter one wit whether he likes me or not."

"You are so dang anti-social," Solace teased. "You even deleted yourself from Spacebook. People back home think you're dead. Besides, as far as Humes, you don't know what you're missing."

"No I don't, and I plan to keep it that way," Port

insisted.

Bliss admired Port's stick-to-it attitude, but personally she liked to remain more open minded. Love, or even lust, shouldn't be shackled by fear, or whatever seemed to be holding Port back. And even for Faes, time wasn't infinite.

She recalled her previous meetings with Nathaniel Winston Calhoun. Their time together had been brief, but she'd felt a connection, some of it quite tingly in all the right places. He hadn't remained long at their open house, but the night she danced with him at the Country Club, and he held her in his arms, had really sparked something deep inside her. Too bad their romantic evening had also been a setup to take down Mr. Smith, the Rep who had been running the show at the time. Spending most of the night in warrior-mode, with or without wings, she hadn't been able to enjoy his company to the fullest. Of course, she hadn't been assigned to Earth to party.

Since that time, Nathaniel had been informed two groups of otherworldly beings were Earth-side—and she was one of them. The Fae being the Earth's ally, the Reptiles their enemy with possible plans to takeover or destroy his precious clocks. Their commander and chief, Mother Nature, indicated Dr. Calhoun had taken it all in stride which seemed impossible, leaving Bliss waiting for the other shoe to drop.

As an astrophysicist, perhaps Nathaniel could more easily accept the idea of extraterrestrial life forms. She sure hoped so. Something about him got her heart racing and her hormones jumping, and it wasn't just his analytical mind. She suspected a whole different persona lurked behind the work-a-day façade he presented to the world. Being an empath, she often got flashes of what lay beneath the surface of those around her. Maybe he would turn out to be a bit of a mad scientist—in a fun way. Or better yet a bad scientist—in a naughty way.

Chapter Two

With only minutes to spare, Bliss entered the National Institute of Standards and Technology building. Just inside the door, Nathaniel waited for her. Tall and broad-shouldered, he wore his white lab coat unbuttoned with a casual coolness not easily attained in such garb. His data profile emphasized his brilliant mind, omitting the fact it came housed in a body more suited for physical activity than jotting down complex formulas on a white board. The collarless linen shirt he sported beneath the white apparel appeared irresistibly soft, and she couldn't help wanting to run her hands over the material.

Remaining silent, he handed her a visitor's pass. Because they hadn't spoken since he'd been given the classified information regarding what they faced and what she was, Bliss worried they may have lost the fragile connection she'd felt before.

"Good morning. I'm terribly excited to finally see what makes things tick around here."

Based on his lack of response, her attempt at humor might have been spoken in the language of her ancestors. He just kept staring at her through those horn-rimmed glasses as if she were a lab experiment—the results still pending. Staring and staring, with the most captivating blue eyes she'd seen this side of the Parsean galaxy.

"So is there somewhere we might talk privately?" she prompted.

He shook his head as if coming out of a trance, and a swatch of his dark hair dipped down over his forehead. "Sure. I'm sorry. Follow me."

They ended up in a cozy conference room outfitted with a long table and several comfy chairs. She leaned one hip on the edge of the smooth expanse of polished wood. He took up residence at a safe distance just inside the door.

"Are we okay here?" she asked.

"Yes, no, I don't know. Why didn't you tell me what was going on, and not only who you are, but what you are?"

"Hadn't been given the go ahead by HQ. I'm sorry if it took you by surprise."

"Surprise… A nearby lightning strike, that takes a body by surprise, and would pale in comparison. I feel like I was thrown and stomped on by my most trusted horse."

His sudden cowboy colloquialism was unexpected, and extremely sexy, pushing him up higher on the alpha male scale. Then it occurred to her he wouldn't be this upset if being partners didn't matter to him—at least a little bit.

"Well, now you know. So what do you think? Talk to me." With caution, she used her talent for calming frightened creatures and attracting males.

His shoulders relaxed, and he stepped closer. "I'm fascinated, of course. But I'd hoped…"

What was it with the unfinished sentences? Did the man think she might be psychic as well as an empath? "I can't read minds, Nathaniel. What did you hope?"

"I was going to ask you out. But now…"

She couldn't help but roll her eyes. "But now…what? You're killing me here."

Easing forward, he studied her face, his expression one of searching, as well as fascination. Then as if she were made of porcelain, he reached out with one hand and gently glided his fingertips downward from her temple to her chin. There was nothing unfinished about the sensation spreading through her from head to toe. A sensation she hadn't felt in a long time. It ended up teasingly and pleasingly in her belly. Hands now pressed against his solid chest, which felt carved from the table she leaned against, Bliss stared back into those blue, blue eyes, the color of a midsummer Solstice sky.

"Would you like to go out with me?" he asked, as if the idea seemed impossible.

"Why wouldn't I?"

"Because you're an…"

Here we go again. "An alien, a space creature, an entity from the great beyond. You can say it, I won't be offended. Besides, you're missing the point. The main thing is I'm a female. And yes, I'd like to go out with you."

A quirky little smile relaxed his mouth. "I definitely didn't miss that particular point." He pushed his glasses up farther on his nose, an action seeming more of habit than necessity. "A man would have to be blind to do so."

She dialed back her allure mechanism, which he didn't appear to need, and as she inhaled a deep breath, she noticed he smelled like mountain air and fresh mowed hay. What was up with that? She enjoyed it, but here on his home-turf, she'd figured he'd reek of mustiness or some kind of odiferous laboratory fragrance. She seemed to keep underestimating him or at least misinterpreting him.

The first time they met, she'd expected a frail pale geek, not a tantalizing hunk. He wasn't a muscle-bound jock who looked like he lived at the gym, but rather he was tall and lanky, with the broad shoulders and narrow hips of a Soccer Pro—or on her planet, a three dimensional air jockey. She could watch those bad boys for hours.

"Does this mean you've come to terms regarding where I come from."

"I'm not sure what you mean by terms. And I really don't know where you come from other than *out there*." He waved his hand around in the air for emphasis. "I've had sufficient time to digest the concept, of course, but there's still too much undiscovered data to come to a conclusion. But then we all have secrets."

"Do we now?" Like many a dark superhero she suspected Dr. Calhoun had an alter ego. Was there a secret cavern nearby, and someone special waiting to help him carryout his clandestine activities? "Have you been briefed on why I'm here, and what we're up against?"

"Again yes. And again, still working on it. I try to keep an open mind. After all, I'm a big supporter of SETI. Did a "tour of duty" at the Lick Observatory for my postgraduate work."

Lick, such a nice four letter word. And in her mind, one that did not conjure telescopes and long boring hours of record keeping with hopes of alien contact.

"So you see," he continued, now leaning against

the doorjamb, arms crossed over his chest. "I certainly believe in the potential for you to exist."

She had to laugh at that, and her thoughts snapped back on track. Maybe he had more of a sense of humor than she'd given him credit for.

"Sounds like a good start."

He gave a little nod. "If you'll follow me, we can take the facility tour for which you have so long and so patiently awaited." Well-deserved sarcasm flavored his statement. She hadn't been patient at all.

Holding the door open, he allowed her to precede him into the hallway. His height, a few inches above hers, equaled another mark on the plus side of the tally. Like Solace, Bliss favored tall men.

As they silently traversed a long passageway, another employee wearing a lab coat came toward them. "Good morning Dr. Calhoun," the man greeted as they intersected. "Morning Dr. Simmons," Nathaniel replied.

"Your doctorate is in astrophysics, right?" she said, trying to get a conversation going. His background file having been required reading, she already knew the answer, but there was still the expunged juvie record which left his childhood info a little sketchy, but extremely intriguing.

"Yes. I also have a PhD in microbiology and neurobiology."

Oh yeah, be still my heart. Her doctor was a triple threat man. Bliss marveled to think one person could be so intelligent, so gifted. She could claim to be good at what she did too, but most of it demanded physical endurance and skillsets not requiring a bucket-load of math. She'd gotten through chemistry and physics on a wing and a prayer. And although she didn't fully understand these advanced theories, she could listen for hours to someone else talking about them.

The hall ended in a set of sturdy doors. She rated them a seven-out-of-ten as far as security worthiness. Nathaniel pressed his palm against a panel on the right. The light above the doors flashed from red to green, and the locks clicked open.

The room they entered came as surprise. She expected a clock, what she saw resembled a clock explosion. Shiny metal pipes and parts were balanced one on top of another in seemingly illogical order, the entire mass highlighted with a rainbow of colored wires and loops of electrical cords. It towered from floor to ceiling, housed in a stark room resembling an unfinished basement.

"Where are the hands and face?"

He glanced at her, his brow creased. "There aren't any. We don't use it to tell time."

"No, of course not. Okay, I'm a little lost here. It's a clock that doesn't tell time.

"Correct. It tells us the exact length of a second so we can calibrate other clocks around the world and determine if they're running fast or slow. We're not marking time, we're actually defining it. Without our accuracy, there goes the power grids, digital television, the internet, timestamps for financial transactions. Time is the most measured quantity on earth."

She had to agree with him there. Humes seemed addicted to time. They were forever carrying or wearing devices telling them the precise time here and elsewhere in their world. For the Fae, time moved more slowly, their lifespan covering hundreds of years. Other than the changing of the seasons, they tended not to worry so much about time.

She worked her face into an expression of fascination, because after all, what he told her was important—at least here on Earth. But where she came from, it would be labeled old hat. *I mean come on, it wasn't as if these folks had finally discovered high energy supersymmetry or something. They were still hashing out String theory vs M theory. They had so many wonderful breakthroughs waiting for them.*

"It will only lose one second in three-hundred million years," he added, his expression begging her to be impressed.

"Well, all right then. That really is something." Had to give them credit for that one at least.

He ran one hand along the copper tubing. "Time, space, and gravity. That's pretty much what it's all about." He had artistic hands, expressive yet masculine. She pictured those long supple fingers flying over the keys of piano—or simply reaching to hold her hand.

"Another difference from the NIST F1 clock is the temperature at which it operates."

Shifting her gaze back to his face, she forced herself to listen to his words.

"The F1 cruises along at a comfortable 80 degrees Fahrenheit. The F2 functions best at -316 degrees Fahrenheit."

"Why the difference?"

"Colder atoms lower the background radiation with which the machine has to contend, and slower atoms mean longer measurements can be taken."

"So maintaining the correct temperature is crucial," she mused aloud. "Could be all important if someone had tampering with the clock in mind."

"Yes, it would be a consideration." He stood a little taller, like a man ready to protect his own. "I'm aware of what happened at NOAA. Do you really think this facility could be a target?"

"It's hard to say what the Reps have in mind. The only thing we're sure about is they're cooking up something. The Jet Propulsion Lab in California took a hit last week, the apparent purpose being the disruption of NASA's Deep Space Network. Fortunately, the Fae Warriors stationed out there contained the attack with minimal damage. East coast activity has picked up as well, so we need to be prepared."

"Fae Warriors," he said, with a sparkle of amusement in his eyes. "I keep forgetting you are one. You seem so..."

"Normal?" she put in. "Well you haven't seen me in Fae mode."

"I'd like too," he admitted. "If you ever need a quiet place to fly around, I've got a little patch of land outside of town. You're welcome there anytime."

Now that idea had merit, especially as a place for Noodge to run wild. "Sounds great. How about tomorrow? It's Saturday, are you free?" Better strike while the asteroid was hot.

Dr. Calhoun's eye's widened, whether from surprise or fear she couldn't tell.

"That'd be great, Miss Goodeve."

He seemed sincere, and this time she felt genuine emotion climb over the wall he'd apparently built around his feelings.

"You can call me Bliss. We're partners you know."

"Yes, of course. And please call me Nate."

Nate. His nickname struck a pleasing chord. Much less stuffy and bookish than Nathaniel. Just as she suspected, another man did exist behind the glasses and lab coat.

****

Their tour completed, Nate watched Bliss drive away.

She had agreed to a visit tomorrow. He hadn't expected his casual offer would be so quickly and enthusiastically accepted, especially not by the most beautiful woman he'd ever met. Bliss—even her name promised happiness. And discovering she came from another planet slam-dunked the growing infatuation he'd felt for her. Didn't every astrophysicist dream of such a reality? But he couldn't tell anyone. No problem. He had plenty of practice keeping secrets, and in fact liked the idea of not sharing who she was with anyone else.

Bliss seemed interested in his work. Probably prompted by her military involvement and nothing personal. What would she think of his other projects? To the outside world, he guessed they weren't as exciting as the clocks. They were important to him though, and lately, he'd decided to do what made him happy.

He'd spent two years trying to make his ex-fiancée happy. He'd even paid for her education, quite the big deal when you are talking CU Boulder. He'd indulged her and her friends with parties at his place, cleaning up the mess they usually left behind. He even paid to have her teeth straightened, and financed her frequent trips to the salon for nails and hair. Admittedly high maintenance, he figured you got what you paid for.

After graduation, she took off to Europe with some young jock. One who offered her a much lower IQ, and what she mistakenly thought was a much bigger family fortune. If she only knew.

After his fiancée left, he realized love didn't come with a price tag to be bought, but it did come at a hefty price if the person broke your heart. Being a fast learner, and having been severely burned, he didn't intend to conduct anymore experiments involving love—even in the name of science.

Still, he couldn't get Bliss out of his mind. He especially liked her glorious hair, burnished copper, a flash of autumn on a perfect fall day. When he'd danced with her at the Country Club, and held all six-feet of her curvy, heavenly scented body in his arms, he'd toyed with the idea of giving love another chance.

Then she'd suddenly taken off into the night and old wounds of the heart, barely-healed, stung with remembered pain. Later, he'd discovered their evening at the Club had been a cover for some kind of a mission she was on and never told him about. He'd felt confused and used. That's the real reason why he kept putting off her tour. But her persistence had worn him down, and discovering her alien status hadn't hurt either.

In the future, he supposed, they might be spending a considerable amount of time together. He should play it cool. And he mustn't be tricked into dropping his shields, or doing something stupid, like falling for her. Love was illogical. As a scientist, he knew such an emotional condition made no sense. Unfortunately, as a man, it made all the sense in the world.

****

"You look like the cat who ate the swallow, or however that goes," Portence teased, from across the main room at their office. The facility, rented out as the Green Goddess Environmental Research Agency, was a cover and war room for their mission.

Not caring what anyone thought, Bliss couldn't stop grinning. "I've a date with Dr. Calhoun tomorrow to visit his *patch of land* as he calls it. Probably just a cabin in the woods, but it will be fun to get out of town."

"Can we come too?" Solace whined. "Being surrounded by the chaos of the city is driving me crazy."

"Definitely not. You have your own Hume to keep you happy. Tanner will take you camping or something if you need a great outdoors fix."

"Did he seem comfortable with the new intel thrown at him?" Port asked. A banana Popsicle in one hand and a laser marker in the other, she turned to study today's updates on the Mother board.

Most crime teams and special op groups had a murder board. The Fae Warriors' high-tech ethereal screen floated five feet off the ground and came mysteriously linked to Mother Nature. Due to these facts, it seemed only right to call theirs the Mother board. But regardless of the name, it remained all about murder.

"I'm happy to report," Bliss informed them, "he's thrilled I'm Fae. He's a brainiac, but I'm betting he could hold his own in a fight."

"Sounds like we've got the brains and brawn covered with our two Hume partners," Solace teased. "Wonder what that leaves for you Port? Maybe someone who can cook or sing pretty."

Solace ducked the laser pen rocketing toward her head.

"Play nice," Bliss ordered.

Apparently, the role of peacekeeper had fallen upon her shoulders today. Not an easy job. And one which rotated around between the three of them. They looked identical, but their personalities were as diverse as their hair color.

"You're too starry-eyed to be issuing orders, Bliss," Port declared, reaching for another pen. "You're a warrior, snap out of it."

"Oh stop pestering her," Solace came to Bliss' rescue. "I think you're jealous because you declared yourself a Hume-free zone, and now you're itchy and beginning to regret that decision."

"Not true," Port huffed.

"It's okay." Bliss grabbed a bottle of water from the little fridge. "You can't bait me into a bad mood. Nate, that's what he prefers to be called, drives me crazy with his scientific lingo."

"Well speaking of science," Port prodded, "what about the clocks, remember the clocks?"

"They already have the security beefed up," Bliss reported. "And I suggested they go on permanent lock down as far as visitors. Being housed in a cement room with few entrances or exits, it would be pretty hard to get to them."

"So, if not Bliss' clock as a target, any thoughts on what the Reps will hit next?" Solace asked.

"If it was me," Port theorized, "I'd be tired of this hit and run stuff they've been pulling. Not one of their missions across the country has been successful because they're lacking in numbers. I'd be working on something more complex, a new plan of attack for when I had more men. Or something more simple, requiring only one. We can't rule out suicide bombers. Either way, they'll need to make inroads soon and build up their troops, or eventually we'll have enough Fae Warriors here to wipe them out completely."

"It does seem odd neither the Reps nor Fae are arriving in greater number," Solace agreed.

"Did you hear from Mother today? Did she say anything about our male Fae warriors being reassigned to the earth anytime soon?" Bliss dropped down into a chair, and leafed through the paperwork on the table.

"Making strides, but still occupied with the battle on Cronos 12," Port supplied.

"Today, we decided to concentrate on how the Reps are funding their operations." Solace took to a chair across from Bliss. "Mother is checking off-planet for the person behind the invasion, but the pile of money you saw at Jones' place had to come from somewhere."

Bliss nodded in agreement. "He could buy a lot of loyalty with that much currency. Organize the Reps assigned to this area. And here's a terrible thought. What if he recruits Humes? They wouldn't know underneath he's an alien just as happy to kill and eat them as to look at them."

"It's a possibility. Their transformation serum has been updated," Port said, "and they're blending in better than ever. And without the side-effects Smith suffered, they have longevity on their side too." She highlighted a few items on the board. "We do have one new situation which could be related to Rep activity."

"And specifically to Jones I hope." Bliss waited with mixed emotions. She wanted nothing more than to track down their green-blooded enemy. But if Jones were involved, it would be good news for them, and probably be bad news for someone else.

"It *could* be tied to our favorite enemy," Port agreed. "Yesterday morning, the Boulder authorities picked up a young woman near the Boulder County Sheriff's office. She's in shock, so they aren't able to procure a coherent statement from her. And the few words she did utter were in Russian, which explains why we're having trouble tracking her down. She didn't appear to be severely injured, but her clothing had blood on it from two different sources.

"One sample matched the girl, the other belonged to another female, also a human. Neither has been reported missing. I picked up samples this morning for testing here, but when we ran it through, we got the same results—two female humans, no identification."

No one knew where Mother had come up with the Rapid-Hit machine, costing $250,000 dollars, and no one really cared or dared to ask. The self-contained identification system, no larger than a standard printer, could take a cheek swab and make a DNA match in 90 minutes or less. Bliss wondered if Homeland Security might have some missing equipment.

"We've got a third sample overlooked by the Boulder CSI team," Port added. "It's Rep blood. I found it on her clothes when I checked her belongings at the police station. I'm sure the Humes took the green color to be paint, or part of the design of her blouse. They wouldn't be looking for green blood."

"The young woman received a proper and thorough

physical," Solace added, grabbing up a manila envelope from the table. "Apparently, she's around seventeen but looks about twelve." Retrieving a photo, she handed it over to Port to transfer to the board."

"Poor thing." Bliss' heart went out to her. "Where is she now?"

"At a safe house," Solace assured. "We haven't gone to see her. We thought your empath skills would be vital when we meet."

"Yes, of course. Have they found any mutilated bodies?" Bliss braced for the answer.

"No, thank Jupiter," Solace said. "Nothing like when Smith controlled the area."

"Investigating the seedier locations around town might yield some information." Port suggested. "There's been a few overdoses in the alleys near the Pearl Street Mall, and even more trouble on the outskirts of town—unusual for Boulder. And all of the deaths involve a drug new to the ATF. The rapid half-life makes it hard to detect, but we lucked out, and the ME found traces of said drug in the girl, meaning she's had contact with a Rep and the drug. There has to be a tie-in."

"Maybe they're bringing the drug in from Russia," Solace commented, "and using young women as mules. Illegal drugs would be a nice moneymaking side-business. We know there are Reps infiltrating all across the globe. Jones could have buddies stationed anywhere."

"We should go undercover." Bliss suggested. "Night people won't talk to cops, but a few working girls should be able to poke around without raising eyebrows amongst the homeless and local clientele."

She glanced at Noodge as he slept on his special bed in the back hallway. "Maybe we should take Noodge if we decide to go out at night." At the sound of his name, the still sleeping Rapran whimpered and pumped his legs as if running free in a dream. "He'd be able to tell if any lizard-brains have been in the area lately. But I suppose he might be a liability if the Reps get wind of him."

"It's a hard choice," Port agreed. "The Hairball is a terrific addition to our arsenal, but he's not what I'd call a secret weapon."

"Speaking of weapons, it might be a good idea to recharge our particle lasers tonight," Solace suggested. "We haven't used them in a while. They may be low from sitting around."

"When can we interview the victim?" Bliss asked. "I can use some soothing techniques or a full-blown empathy-mind meld, help her feel safe, and maybe find out what she knows or at least what she saw. We need to figure out the connection between her, the drug, and the Reps."

"There's no time like the present for the interview," Port said, "but let's schedule our girls' night out for tomorrow evening. That'll give us time to let Mother in on our plans, and Solace can run it by Tanner and see if there's anything new on his radar."

"I suggest," Solace said, gaining her feet, "after we interview our victim, we go browse the secondhand stores, and come up with some working girl outfits."

Bliss checked her purse for cash. "Always up for a shopping trip."

"Oh brother." Port shook her head. "We really need a bigger car."

Chapter Three

Their little cross-over vehicle rolled to a stop beneath the secluded portico. Bliss leaped out first and led the way. Of the three of them, this afternoon's activities would take the heaviest toll on her. That's why she'd been gearing herself up for the meeting all the way across town. Now she needed to get this over with while she felt pumped and ready.

"Maybe we should go first," Solace said, glancing over at Portence as they both tried to keep up.

Bliss shook her head. "Thanks guys. I'll be fine. My aura should be the first one she feels. If this is going to work, she needs to attach to me." This time, she ran the show. Maybe she couldn't draw down lightning like Port, or command the air like Solace, but her special powers were going to make it possible to speak with their unknown subject.

On the way over, Port had notified the PD they were on the way to the safe house, and the update they received stated the girl remained catatonic, hadn't spoken or eaten for nearly two days. There were signs of sexual abuse, but she seemed in good health otherwise. Bliss hoped she could coax her back to reality, and help her to heal.

Reaching the huge, black front door, she halted. With her sisters at her back, Bliss grabbed and put to use the heavy brass door knocker while she read the letters stenciled in gold on the beveled glass side panel. *Marx Brothers Mortuary/ Al, Ben, and Carl Marx proprietors.* Cripes, that seemed wrong on so many levels. No wonder they went out of business.

Setting up the safe house in a non-operating funeral parlor had been a stroke of genius. It might sound horrible, but the building met all the requirements—a first class alarm system, camera monitors in all but a few rooms, a small apartment with all amenities, and best and most creepy of all, people could be brought in and out via a hearse, or coffins. Who'd think to look for live people in a mortuary?

The door finally opened a crack then widened, revealing a young, very much alive, police woman in full uniform. She appeared well-armed and capable, and barely blinked upon seeing the sisters for the first time. *The Sisters of Anu*, Bliss thought with a little rush of pride. Most folks when hit by the trifecta of faces did a double-take. Hopefully the officer's reaction meant she had been thoroughly briefed regarding their arrival.

All three Fae whipped out their top security badges, and offered them up for inspection.

"We're the civilian consultants here to meet with the young woman," Bliss stated.

"Yes, ma'am. I'm Officer Gail Westen. The Commissioner informed us of your intentions. Please come in." She stood back, opening the door wider. "Officers Stanton and Larkin are also on the premises. Under the circumstances we decided an all-female team would be the best idea."

"Under most circumstances an all-female team is the best idea," Port growled, then grinned.

Bliss entered the main waiting area, and

immediately diverted energy to her shields. She couldn't worry about or connect with the dozens of human souls which had passed through this building. Too late to do anything for them other than wish them well. Luckily there didn't seem to be many still hovering about, and she was able to fend them off. The girl, that's where her powers were needed. She supposed, from the victim's point of view, bringing her here hadn't eased whatever horrors prowled around in her mind. That is if she were even aware of her surroundings.

They followed Westen, pausing briefly at the open door to a room cluttered with computer monitors. The uniform behind the sea of equipment glanced at them, acknowledged their presence with a thumbs-up, and went back to concentrating on the flat screens.

Moving on, they reached the door to the apartment.

Westen knocked, announced herself and indicated she had company. Again the door opened a crack, then all the way. The uniform on the other side, small and wiry, had her hand on the butt of a holstered pistol.

"These are the civilians the Commish told us about," Westen said. "We'll leave you alone." I sure hope you can help her," she added, glancing at Bliss.

As the three of them entered, the two officers took their leave. Port shut the door and stood at attention taking up guard position.

Solace hung back too as Bliss eased forward. The girl they'd come to see sat motionless, her skin white enough to have been carved from alabaster, her unblinking stare aimed at the wall rather than the nearby window.

"You're safe now," Bliss said, barely above a

whisper. "We're here to help you." As expected, she got no response. The young woman's aura appeared dim and ragged as if sheltered from the sun and chewed on by rats. Bliss' heart ached for her, but sympathy wouldn't bring her back or help them figure out what had happened to her.

Fortifying their victim's psyche before connecting sounded like a good idea. Eyes squinted in concentration, Bliss surrounded the suffering girl with a gentle green light. Her body relaxed the tiniest bit, and her right hand twitched.

Situated in the middle of the color spectrum, green contained the power of both the physical and spiritual realms, affecting balance, harmony, and healing. Shifting to a golden hue, Bliss strengthened the young woman's nervous system, awakening mental inspiration. Ending with indigo, for purification and freeing the mind, she felt they were ready to begin the empath connection she'd come to perform.

Easing into the chair across from her, Bliss braced herself mentally. It was now or never. Eyes closed she willed her own aura to encompass the young woman. It didn't hurt, not yet. It only felt as if she were being stretched thin and couldn't take a deep breath. Then the girl's aura melded with her own, and the pain came in waves, washing over her, crushing her, sucking up what little breath she'd had in her lungs. The poor thing was terrified, her mind locked down to prevent her from going insane.

What had sent her over the edge? Now fully mind-melded, Bliss waited for the visions to clear. So that was it—she'd seen one of their enemy—in reptile form. And worse yet, he'd captured and eaten the girl traveling with her as they were fleeing for their lives. Bliss opened her eyes, and choked back the bile rising in her throat. Although a seasoned warrior, the vision turned her stomach. Because this girl had survived at the other's expense, guilt rode hand in hand with the horror.

Tightening her grip on the arms of the chair, Bliss faced down the mental monsters, capturing the revolting and negative emotions and forcing them into the ethereal silver box she created. The gist of what happened would be retained, minus the reptile, and seen as if from a distance. It would no longer be a threat to the girl. She left a smidgen of regret. Good or bad, actions had consequences, a lesson learned. And she left sorrow for the lost girl. The importance of mourning shouldn't be discounted.

Closing and locking the shiny little thought-box, she tucked it away in a corner of the girl's mind where it would forever remain hidden. Now the recent events could be discussed without brutalizing the girl's consciousness. Bliss registered the pertinent information too, but hearing this young woman's take on what happened would be more helpful.

"You're safe now," Bliss chanted, again drawing deep on her own energy. "Come back. We will protect you."

After a few minutes, which felt like forever, a shudder ran through the girl, a mewling sound escaped her lips, and her expression took on new life. Bliss poured white light into her subject, infusing her with strength as their energies mingled, filling the empty aura with her own light.

"Come back to us," she commanded.

Haunted brown eyes locked onto hers and widened in wonder. While their minds connected, the girl would be viewing Bliss in her spirit-state—meaning full-blown wings, a gossamer gown, and glowing tribal tattoos.

"Are you an angel?" the girl whispered.

"No, little one," Bliss replied, patting her hand. No matter how you sliced it, the Sisters of Anu were far from angelic. "Just a friend."

Slowly breaking their connection, so as not to jolt or injure the girl, Bliss took a few deep breaths to regain her own equilibrium. Then she prepared for what would inevitably happen to her subject when she terminated one of her empath links.

The girl pitched forward out of the chair. Bliss caught and eased her down to her knees, leaving her head and shoulders resting in Bliss' lap. She stroked the tangled head of hair while the girl wept. "There, there. You're safe now," she repeated the mantra of the day. "Everything will be okay. Can you tell me your name?"

The girl glanced up through tear-filled eyes. "Oksana. My name is Oksana."

Bliss urged the young woman off her knees and back into the chair. "Well then, Oksana, I need to ask you some questions. Will that be all right?"

"I can't remember how I got here." She sat up straighter and blinked a few times as if coming out of a trance. Bliss' question apparently forgotten.

"Where were you before coming here?" she prodded.

"I remember the before time, when they kept us locked in the room, but I don't know exactly where we were." Her breathing quickened and her eyes grew wide as if in surprise or terror. "I remember my cousin, Yana. I remember the things they made us do..." Her voice faded to silence, and she slumped forward, covering her face with her hands.

Grabbing a nearby box of tissues, Bliss set it in Oksana's lap. Then she dared to graze the fingertips of one hand across the back of the girl's wrist. Energy burst directly from Bliss to Oksana sending a visible jolt through the girl even as it anchored her mind to Bliss', making her temporarily more compliant.

"Was Yana with you when you ran away?" Bliss prayed Yana wasn't the girl who had been eaten.

"No, it was Dixie. She's dead. Poor Dixie. She came from here, in America. She spoke good English, tried to teach us. She came up with idea for us to escape."

Tears began again in earnest, yet Oksana seemed more in control, more focused, and Bliss intended to keep her in the present.

"Why don't we find you some food?" she suggested, glancing over at Solace.

As if seeing the room for the first time, Oksana peered around, cringing back in her chair as her gaze fell on Solace and Portence.

"It's okay. They're my sisters," Bliss reassured, reeling in the girl's attention.

"Yes, here to help me." Oksana parroted back the words Bliss sent her by telepathy.

Solace left the room in search of food, and Port held position at the door.

"Now then," Bliss said, steering the interrogation to more familiar ground, "where are you from?"

"I come from Dubovka. In Russia," she added,

when Bliss didn't acknowledge the name of the city.

"It is beautiful back home, on the right bank of the Volga. But it is a poor town, and they promised Yana and me a good life here in America. A good life and enough money to send back to help our families."

"Who promised you this?"

"Lies. All lies," Oksana said, veering off in her own direction, anger and sadness raising her voice an octave. "They make us do terrible things, with men off the streets, or sometimes with each other. The ones in charged never touched us, they watched, touching themselves. I'm so thankful to be away, but now Dixie is dead, and Yana and Troika still suffer. Troika is but a child."

Bliss took a calming breath hoping Oksana wouldn't pick up on the seething anger she felt for the Reps and their disgusting moneymaking sidelines.

"Sure you don't have any idea where you were being held?" Bliss brought up a map of Boulder on her handheld. But when she showed it to the girl, it made her cry.

"I am stupid," she said, vehemently. "I don't even know where I am. We were all stupid to believe them, stupid to think anyone would care about Yana and me. Stupid to run away with Dixie."

"You are not stupid," Bliss insisted. "And you were running for help, not away. It was a brave thing you did. Believe me I know what it's like to find yourself in alien territory."

"I'm sorry. Everything here is so confusing. We learned the English in school, but here it sounds different, and there are many words I do not know."

"You're doing just fine. Anything you tell me

might help."

Before she could ask another question, Solace returned, her arms full of food—including half a dozen sandwiches, two bags of chips, several diet sodas, and a box of cookies. Oksana's eyes brightened, and although Bliss knew she must be starving, she didn't reach for the food.

Solace placed all of it on the little table at their side. "Go for it girlfriend," she said, handing her a napkin.

Not having to be asked twice, the young woman pounced on the food. "Thank you," she said around a hearty mouthful. "If we complained about the food, they beat us."

"Friggin' lowlifes," Solace snapped. "You'd think they'd take better care of the merchandise."

"You're right," Port put in from across the room. "Maybe there's more going on than meets the eye. The sex-trafficking sounds like quick cash, but also a lot of work for the amount of return."

It made sense. Bringing the women all the way from Russian, and taking care of them would become cumbersome after a while, even if done carelessly. "Dealing the new drug we think might be involved would be an easier source of income, junkies rarely complain or go running to the cops."

"I wonder where they're getting the stuff? The local suppliers and sellers must be pretty unhappy about the Reps taking over their territory," Solace pointed out. "And since we discovered their restaurant hideout, no more laundering their dirty money there. They'll have to come up with a new scheme."

At the mention of the word restaurant, Oksana

perked up.

"At first we were upstairs above a restaurant—a ресторан. There we had plenty to eat. But one day, no warning, they moved the four of us who are left to a kind of boarding house. Long time empty, the new place smelled bad." At the memory, Oksana made a face and wrinkled her nose. "Sometimes the bathroom did not work properly. And the food came not so good, not so plentiful."

"Why did you say 'the four of us who were left'? How many women were there originally?" Bliss asked.

"We came over in a group. I'm not sure how many. They took the others away after a few days. We did not see them again." Oksana began to cry again.

"Don't go there right now," Bliss warned, trying to keep her on track. "You made it out, and you're going to help us rescue the others. "What time of day did you escape?"

"At first light of the morning. We had been out all night working. We took the money profits and ran."

"Did you run toward or away from the mountains?" Bliss asked, hoping to nail down a direction.

"I don't know. Just ran."

"Did you feel the sun on your right shoulder or your left?" Port called out.

Eyes closed, Oksana ran her right hand over her left upper arm. "On here," she said, now wide-eyed and hopeful.

"So they ran south from wherever they were being held," Solace said.

"Do you recall any sounds where you were staying?" Bliss pressed for more.

"Yes. Big trucks, coming and going at all hours. And there were the little planes. They were very noisy, sometimes they would wake us from our sleep."

"Can you recall any shops or street signs nearby? Any small detail might help us know where you were."

"There was the restaurant, with the golden arches, we could see it from the corner where we waited for the men. We thought everything here would be golden. You can't believe what you see on the Internet at school."

"Okay." Solace reconfigured the maps on her handheld. "Now we're getting somewhere. Sounds like they might have been staying near the Municipal airport just off of Valmont Road. Plenty of old warehouses around there to stash them in, and some seedy avenues nearby just right for trolling after sundown. Let's see, there's a McDuck's on Flatiron Parkway, and the Sheriff who picked her up is out of the Baseline Road station. That's all within a five mile radius. Very doable as the crow flies, especially if the crow is terrified and running on adrenalin. Has to be where we look."

"Very good, Oksana," Bliss praised. "You've help us tremendously."

"Please find Yana and Troika," the girl whispered. "You are their only hope."

Chapter Four

After a good night's sleep and a power-smoothie, infused with herbs from her home planet, Bliss felt surprisingly rejuvenated. She also felt obligated to keep her promise to spend the day with Nate. In her absence, Solace and Port were to update their new info, contact Mother, and reconnoiter the area they would visit tonight—when the real action would begin.

"Does he know Noodge is a Rapran?"

"No, Solace," Bliss admitted. She couldn't help but chuckled as she shoved the creature into the backseat of the car and buckled him in. "I just asked if I could bring a pet."

"Should prove interesting." Port gave Noodge a rare pat on the head, and closed the car door. "Try not to bring him back covered in mud."

"Is your personal GPS activated? Solace asked, as Bliss slid behind the wheel.

"You bet, sis. Don't worry. You guys stay on the alert too. The area we're hitting tonight might not be too nice in the light of day either. Are you meeting up with Tanner today, Solace?"

"Yes. A quick check-in and data share, after our recon."

"Any word yet from Colorado Springs and your Hume partner, Port?"

"No, and I wish you guys would quit asking. It just

adds fuel to the fire. I'm as irritated as the cat wranglers of Felinious II. Mother promised I'd hear from him soon, but seeing is believing."

"Sorry, Port. Hang in there. And don't take it out on those around you. It isn't their fault."

"Yeah, yeah, I'll be as sweet as a Venusian sugar plum. You be careful too, and don't lose the fur-ball in the woods."

Following the directions Nate had given her, Bliss headed out for what she hoped would be a day of relaxing and getting to know her partner better.

As the landscape went from city to country, the traffic all but dissolved away, leaving her enjoying the scenery. Noodge gave a good howl as if he were happy to be out of the city too. She lowered the window on his side so he could shove part of his face into the wind like any carnivore worth his salt. She didn't dare lower it all the way for fear he'd rip the seatbelt loose and take off for parts unknown.

Double-checking the directions, she finally spotted the turnoff indicated. As she swung to the left, off the paved road and onto dirt, her pulse quickened. When Nate said he had a little patch of land, she expected one of those mini-ranch homes with five acres attached. She hadn't seen a house or any type of building for miles. Maybe she'd made a mistake, taken a wrong turn. Noodge didn't seem to mind, he continued to suck in the pine-scented country air, his nose going a mile a minute.

Then she saw the *Calhoun Country* sign, carved on a big slab of wood atop an even bigger wooden archway. The ruts and bumps in the road demanded she slow down, and after what seemed longer than the actual ten minutes, she rounded a curve and sucked in a big breath of her own. "My stars and galaxy," she said, braking to a stop and turning off the engine. "It looks like a scene from a western movie."

Constructed of the biggest logs she'd seen this side of the Verde Tree Planet, the ranch house sprawled before her. The covered front porch accommodated five well-used mismatched rocking chairs, and each of the three steps leading up to the front door held a ceramic pot, happily overflowing with petunias. Everything appeared neat and clean, and she couldn't help but wonder if Nate had a girlfriend, or someone who helped to keep the place looking so spit/spot and cheerful.

Leaving Noodge in the car, against his will, she got out, climbed the steps, and using the door knocker, announced her arrival. It sounded quiet as deep space inside, and no one came to answer her summons. Maybe he'd forgotten. She slumped in disappointment as she retraced her steps. Then she heard noises, and her spirit soared. Horses, she heard *horses*.

Fae ears on alert, she ran around the side of the house toward the sound. When she spied the corral, she stopped short—nearly taking a tumble. A cowboy stood in the middle of the paddock, training and lunging a beautiful dun horse. Creeping closer, she took shelter beside the barn, and watched him work. Tall and lean, the man wore a faded blue shirt with the sleeves rolled up, jeans that hugged his perfect ass as if they'd been made to fit, and a beat up straw cowboy hat sporting a concho studded hatband.

Expertly handling the long whip and lunge line, he turned slowly, putting the mare through her paces. Head up and ears on alert, the mare appeared to be enjoying the exercise, which led Bliss to believe the horse cooperated out of mutual respect and compassionate training. The man came about, and when she saw his face she grabbed the side of the building for support. The tantalizing cowboy was Nate.

****

Nate glanced up and spotted Bliss watching. His heartrate doubled. She'd kept her promise.

"Good girl," he crooned to the mare trying to keep his wits about him. He slowed the horse to a walk, then a halt, and reaching out grasped the lead just below the halter. As he led her to the near side of the workout pen, he tried not to overreact as Bliss ambled over to stand on the other side of the rail fence.

"What a beautiful animal." She gently stroked the mare's face, but her gaze met his head on as they studied one another.

Even with sunglasses and a cowgirl hat, she appeared just as beautiful as that night at the country club. The legs of her low-riding jeans were tucked into cowboy boots, and her knit top, the color of wild Columbines, clung happily to her trim waist and otherwise full figure. A figure he'd like to get to know a whole lot better.

"Hi. I see you found us okay." What a dumb thing to say. Bliss was a full grown woman, and a warrior to boot, of course she could easily follow the directions he'd given her. Like an infatuated twelve-year-old, he wanted to tug on her thick auburn braid to distract her from his silly comment.

"When you said you lived on a patch of land, I never imagined all this," she admitted, glancing around. "It's wonderful."

"Belonged to my Uncle Zebulon Calhoun, and his father before him. Now it's mine, although I'd rather Uncle Zeb lived and breathed, and it still belonged to him."

Giving himself time to think, Nate headed for the barn, the mare in tow. Bliss slipped through the rail fence to walk beside him. After putting Molly in her stall, he removed the halter, grabbed a curry comb and brush, and began grooming her.

"I'm sorry about your uncle. Has he been gone long?" Bliss lounged outside the stall, her folded arms resting on the half-door.

"I reckon it's almost five years now. He pretty much raised me, so our feelings ran deep."

"It's a big place to keep up all by yourself."

"I enjoy it, although it can get a bit lonely. But it's peaceful, and with my lab set up here, that's an advantage. Nobody bothers me."

"Your lab?"

She sounded concerned. Did she think he might be whipping up something dastardly in his spare time?

"I work at the institute to keep body and soul together," he explained. "It forces me to interact with people and keeps me grounded. Otherwise, I'm afraid I'd be content to stay here twenty-four-seven." Dang he hadn't meant for all that to come spewing out. Generally, he kept personal information just that, personal. But for some reason he didn't want secrets between them. "My real love is research of a biological nature," he added, going for broke. "When I'm finished here, I'll give you the grand tour."

"Sounds great. Oh, and I brought the pet I mentioned. He's going to need to get out of the car pretty soon, or there may not be a car left. He's a bit rambunctious."

Nate gave Molly a pat on the rump then eased out of and secured the stall door. Grabbing a wedge of hay from an open bale, he rewarded the animal for a job well done. "We better see to your pet. It's unkind to keep animals confined. Especially on such a pretty day as this."

He walked beside her, inhaling Bliss' scent. So tall and lithe, she reminded him of a thoroughbred. Some horses were known as warmbloods, but by the energy coming off of her, he had a feeling hot-blooded fit her better.

"So what kind of dog did you bring?" he asked as they rounded the tack house and headed for her car.

"Actually it isn't a dog. It's called a Rapran short for Rapacious Ranivorous."

"Ranivorous? It eats frogs?"

"Rapaciously. And snakes and lizards."

Ah, now it made sense. "Lizards. You mean like Reptiles?"

"You got it."

He stopped short, and turned to face her, and his pulse quickened. "Is it otherworldly?"

"Yes…"

Her voice held trepidation, but he couldn't be more excited. Good Lord, he felt as if all his boyhood cosmic dreams were coming true. A beautiful "space lady" at his side, and now an alien creature about to run wild on his property.

"Well, hot damn." He hurried on, leaving her to catch up.

As they approached the car, a magnificent howling

ensued, and the wild and wooly animal visible through the windshield seemed to fill the entire car. Nate glanced over his shoulder. With the barn door closed, and all the horses stalled or in well-fenced runs, they should be safe, and not feel threatened by the beast.

Bliss opened the door a crack and grabbed the stout leash attached to the Rapran's collar. "Now you behave yourself, Noodge," she ordered before opening the door wider.

He exploded out of the car, bounced up and down, and gave another hair-raising howl.

"Sit, Noodge," Bliss commanded.

The huge shaggy ball of energy obeyed instantly, staring up at Bliss with adoring eyes. Gees, he hoped he didn't appear as smitten when he looked at her.

"This is Nate," Bliss introduced. "Let him smell your hand," she instructed.

He tentatively reached out. If Bliss hadn't been there, he might have refused such a request. Yet, without any notion as to why, he trusted her. It didn't make sense. First of all, she was a female, and he had no great track record there. And secondly she wasn't even human. Of course, that fact could possibly be a point in her favor.

Noodge stared at him with golden eyes, a row of large white teeth clearly visible in his huge mouth. His trust wavered, and he fought the urge to jerk his hand away. Even in his wildest dreams he'd never imagined such a creature. The beast sniffed, then slobbered and licked his hand with a tongue the size of a turkey platter.

"Once he has your scent, and knows you're a friend, he'll protect you with his life if so ordered."

Bliss' words struck deep. Suddenly the true seriousness of what he'd been told about invaders from another world, and the ultimate takeover of the human race, hit him full force. Until now, the hard to assimilate scenario had sounded farfetched, like the latest Hollywood offering. But standing here with Bliss and Noodge on his own property, it became reality. Still, despite the horror of it all, what a golden opportunity.

"He's remarkable," Nate murmured, wiping his hand on his jeans. "Any chance I can get a blood sample for analysis? Or just some hair. I'd love to check out his DNA."

"Maybe. We'd better let him go for a run first."

"Does he come when you call?" he asked.

"Most of the time."

That didn't sound good.

"Just kidding." Bliss followed her assurance with a delightfully girlish laugh. "He'll behave."

"Let's take him to the south pasture. It's fenced, and there aren't any horses grazing there today."

"Terrific. Noodge would love it, wouldn't you boy? Living in the city we don't get out much."

"I can only imagine."

As a community, Boulder could be a tad controlling and rule obsessed. An entity unto itself, known by some as the United States of Boulder. When lost in their own little universe, the residents were not always accepting to all who would join them.

"Rules and regs are not my cup of Joe either," he admitted, "but so far I've managed to balance the job in town with living free out here." The 120 acres he called home were a part of what made him who he was.

"Is that why the two personas? The staid scientist vs the rough and ready cowboy?"

"Yep. It seems to work for me."

He turned and led the way to the pasture. Growing up, he hadn't always obeyed the law. He counted himself fortunate the foolish mistakes of his youth hadn't led him to worse offenses and serious jail time. He had a record with several minor infractions and one major federal offense, and as his current job came under the control of the U.S. Department of Commerce, this type of detrimental information needed to be kept under wraps. Thanks to his uncle's insistence and close friendship with someone in Washington D.C., Nate's juvie record remained a thing of the past.

With Bliss and Noodge at his side, they reached the gate. He opened it and ushered them through. "Okay, Noodge. It's all yours."

As if understanding every word, the Rapran bounded forward, jumping and twisting in the air with a joy he'd often seen in his horses as they ran free after a long spate of winter.

"I think you have a friend for life," Bliss said with a laugh.

"I hope so." Nate replied, with Bliss more in mind than Noodge.

****

After a lengthy and exuberant run, they secured Noodge in the indoor arena where he had room to play, plenty of water, and shelter from the afternoon heat. Retrieving a comb from her pocket, she tried to detangle a bit of Noodge's abundant shaggy coat, and not meaning to she pulled out a large tuft. He didn't seem to notice or mind.

Gini Rifkin

"Thank you," Nate said, as she handed the fur to him. "I can't wait to see this under a microscope."

"I think he's actually done-in." Bliss gave the beast a final pat on the head. "I've never seen him so spent since his arrival," she added, ambling along beside Nate to the main ranch house.

"Where exactly did he arrive from?" Nate asked.

"I don't know where he came from originally. Mother rescued his species from a cruel fate and took them to Remedium 5 to heal, and—"

"Where's that, where's that," he interrupted like an excited child.

Bliss couldn't help but find Nate's enthusiasm for all things extraterrestrial endearing. Hopefully she made the top of his list.

"It's hard to explain without a map," she admitted, and laughed. "It's a *big* Multiverse."

In tandem, they ran up the steps to the house. He opened the front door, allowing her to enter first. The log home, cool and inviting, boasted comfortable looking overstuffed couches and chairs gathered around a huge floor-to-ceiling rock fireplace. Off to the right, the area opened into a large kitchen, with modern appliances and a row of windows along the wall accommodating the sink. It smelled like pine and fresh baked bread.

"You missed lunch, Natty," a male voice accused.

Although the words had been innocuous, they halted Bliss in her tracks.

"Buenos dias, mujer hermosa. Where are your manners, Natty, introduce me."

The small man across the room flashed a welcoming grin, and her concern dissolved away. He

50

wore the required jeans and boots, and a western shirt with silver snaps rather than buttons. Little bucking horses were embroidered along the yoke. His skin, the color of old hickory, showed creases no doubt earned by age and sun, and he sported a neatly trimmed mustache, his gray-streaked, long hair held back in a leather thong.

"This *beautiful lady* is Bliss Goodeve. Bliss, this is Alfonso, my best friend and vaquero. He tries to keep me out of trouble and claims it's a fulltime job."

Alfonso...Mars bars, she nearly freaked. For a moment she thought he was going to say Alfred. Close enough. Her super-hero alter-ego illusion just jumped off the charts.

Alfonso proudly crossed the room, took the hand she extended, and to her surprise he bowed and kissed the back of it. "Welcome to Casa Calhoun. It is an honor to meet you. Natty so rarely has guests these days."

So, he didn't have a regular girlfriend. At least not one he brought here. "Thank you for such a gracious welcome. *Natty* and I are working together on a project, so I hope to come back again sometime."

Nate rolled his eyes at her use of his nickname.

"Speaking of work, this way to my lab. Oh, and Alfonso, there's a rather large dog in the covered arena. Best left to himself I imagine."

"I got it, boss. How about I make you both a sandwich and bring it to you," the older man called after them.

"She doesn't eat meat," Nate called back. "Better make hers peanut butter."

Bliss glanced at Nate, her eyes widened in surprise.

"At the Country Club, you were happy because the hor d'oeuvres offered so many vegetarian selections."

"How thoughtful of you to remember."

"Alfonso will have a hard time wrapping his head around the idea," he said, as he turned and watched the older man walked away, all the while shaking his head. "But then there are so many things about you that are extraordinary."

"Not to mention extraterrestrial."

"I don't think he's ready for that yet," Nate said, walking onward. "But knowing him, he'll figure something unusual is going on.

"We should check with Mother before you say anything," she suggested. Nate nodded in agreement as they reached what appeared to be a mudroom on the far side of the house. He tugged on a coat hook, forcing it downward, and a small panel popped open revealing a pad of numbers. He keyed in a code, and a full-size door, resembling part of the wall, clicked opened. They stepped inside, and the door closed automatically at their backs.

The scrupulously clean room measured at least twenty by twenty feet, and had whitewashed walls lit during the day by skylights. Two rows of deep shelving held quality equipment, sparkling clean, and ready for use. On the large counter top, beakers, Bunsen burners, Petrie dishes, and glass tubes were assembled in planned disarray as if one discovery had led to another and another. A large whiteboard stood to one side covered in formulas as foreign to her as the language spoken on Rangle 3.

A generator kicked on catching her attention. "What's that?"

"The room is climate controlled," Nate explained, as he donned a white lab coat and set his Stetson aside, transforming himself from cowboy to scientist. He handed her a coat too, which she tugged on and buttoned.

"It also has an air evacuation system should something dangerous get loose in here."

"Something dangerous?"

"I'm experimenting with Corynebacterium pseudotuberculosis, also known as Dry Land Distemper." He handed her a pair of safety glasses, and donned a set as well.

"Yikes," she said, quickly taking and putting on the latex gloves he handed out next.

"Don't worry, it isn't zoonotic. Not transmittable from horses to humans." Then he took a quick step back, an expression of panic crossing his face. "What if it's transmittable to Faes?"

"It's okay." She placed a hand on his arm. "We've been thoroughly checked-out six ways to Sunday. If you're immune, we're immune. We have our own weaknesses and diseases of course, but they aren't transmittable to humans. And vise-versa."

He exhaled a big breath, and his shoulders relaxed as if in relief. "I don't even want to think what this disease would do to a human or Fae body."

"What exactly is it?"

"The common name is Pigeon Fever. It affects horses, cattle, goats, etcetera."

"So it's carried by pigeons?"

"No, actually it's transmitted by fly bites, but the infected animal develops large abscesses in the chest wall making him appear to be puffed up like a pigeon.

It can be fatal. A year ago, I lost two horses to the illness, and it also weakened three others. So far it's mostly treated symptomatically, but I'm hoping to find a vaccine or cure."

Latex hand in latex hand, he led her to one of the huge contraptions situated at the other end of the room.

"An electron microscope," she murmured.

"Better," he declared, setting Noodge's hair nearby to be examined later. "It's a superSTEM microscope. According to the news media, there's only three in the world. This is number four. I had it specially made, and I'd like its existence kept quiet if you don't mind."

"Of course." This one piece of apparatus alone had to cost upwards of a million dollars. Not wanting to be nosey, she still needed to be sure some group or person wasn't backing his work. Outside money might be financially helpful, but it could also be dangerous. "Guess your job at the institute pays pretty well for you to be able to have all these great toys to play with."

"Not really. Bought this beauty with my own money. Uncle Zebulon and his ancestors got wealthy from not only this land, but a few parcels up in Leadville and there about. Struck it rich mining silver, and the blessed hole-in-the-ground hasn't played out yet."

"I didn't mean to pry." Now she felt bad for not trusting him, but current conditions put safety above hurt feelings or good manners.

"It's okay. Like I said before. We all have secrets. Yours beat mine though."

Her heart melted. He really didn't mind her non-human status. Through the safety glasses she noticed his blue eyes darken, and he leaned closer. Finally, the kiss she'd been hoping for. Too bad she had to be dressed like a science geek going on a biohaz special op.

"Knock, knock. Time for some food, Natty. You forget to eat too often."

They jumped apart, both breathing faster than normal, and for the first time, Nate almost regretted sharing the pass code to the lab with Alfonso.

Nudging the door open with his shoulder, his friend entered and set a large wooden tray laden with food on a nearby desk. "See you eat it all, mijo. Is the young lady staying the night? I will prepare a room for her."

She sure wanted to stay the night, but not in a separate room. "Actually I must be leaving soon. But thank you, Alfonso, for the food and for the thought."

"Bueno, I will leave the two of you alone then." With a little bow he left, closing the door behind him.

She turned and faced Nate, her breath still coming too fast. Boldly removing his glasses and then her own, she took up where they'd left off, capturing his mouth with hers. The kiss, long and deep, made her stomach flutter and her knees weak. She gripped the lapels of Nate's lab coat and held on tight. One of his hands meandered from her shoulder to her backside, but through all the clothing and lab gear she could barely feel his touch. Lips still devouring his, she eased her hips closer, but again too many layers of fabric thwarted the reaction she'd been going for.

They both broke out laughing. "I believe in safe sex, but this is ridiculous," he said.

She took a step back, and with their latex fingers intertwined, they stared at one another. "I probably should be taking off anyway. Noodge has no doubt revived, and even after eating that big helping of dry cat chow I brought along, he may be getting hungry and bored and into serious trouble out there."

"Cat chow?"

"I know. Weird right? But regardless of his wagging tail and sloppy kisses, dog food upsets his stomach." She needed to ask Mother what his natural prey might be other than lizards and frogs, although on second thought maybe she really didn't want to know."

"Okay, well here. At least take your sandwich to go. You're probably hungry too."

He wrapped the focaccia bread, peanut butter and jam masterpiece in a pristine white linen napkin, and handed it to her. Her stomach grumbled. Once they hit the road, she'd have that gone before they cleared his property line.

"You'll come again soon, I hope. We can go horseback riding. And there's a pond near the stream. Lined with river rock, and with the mild autumn we're having, it's still warm." He tugged at her sleeve. "No lab coats necessary—or swimming suits."

"Sounds...naughty. I like that idea."

Chapter Five

As afternoon shadows lengthened, Port, Solace, and Tanner sat around the table at the Green Goddess Company sharing the results of their morning activities, and taking notes to update Bliss when she returned from Nate's.

"How goes the training and recruiting?" Solace asked.

Port could almost feel the flash of heat generated when Tanner's gaze locked onto her sister's. Apparently he could still make Solace's blue blood boil with just a look. She remembered that feeling—with mixed emotions—and wondered if she would ever experience it again.

"The training is going great," Tanner reported, "but it's getting harder and harder to find qualified men. We have pretty stringent requirements, and then, you know, there's the—oh by the way, you'll be fighting giant lizards thing."

"If anyone can do it, it's you," Solace encouraged, placing a hand on his forearm.

Preparing a unit of men to fight Reptiles had to be dicey, but a challenge Port knew Tanner would meet with flying colors. Solace's Hume embodied the heart and code of a true warrior. She admired that about him. But she knew from experience that approaching the world in black and white could be a tough way to live.

It was a good thing he had Solace to lighten the load and throw a little color at him.

Levering to her feet, Solace went to the fridge and grabbed three sodas, after handing out two she popped the top on hers and sat back down.

"Thanks, babe." Tanner opened his drink and put it to quick use. "What's new with you guys?" he asked, between swallows.

"We reconnoitered the area we'll be visiting tonight." Tapping a finger on the map spread out on the table, Solace indicated the precise location.

"Sure wish you'd let me deploy some of my men to hold the perimeter for you."

Tanner resisted the idea of the three of them going off on their own. Sometimes, Port thought he forgot they were warriors, just like him. "Appreciate the offer," she put in. "But we're not even taking Noodge. If the Reps get wind of anything hinky, they might pull out, or freak out. This could be our only chance to save those two girls."

"Okay. I get it. It's your op. But I think some night maneuvers not too far away might be in order." He didn't look about to change his mind so arguing seemed pointless.

"I'll show you some night maneuvers." Solace leaned sideways, and playfully nudged Tanner's shoulder with hers.

"Do you think they'll try for the Fountain Clock where Bliss' partner works?" Port asked, ignoring their antics. "By now they have to realize the security there has been jacked up, as well as on similar targets."

"Mother reports the number of Reps arriving has reduced down to a trickle." Tanner crumpled his empty pop can, and as if shooting hoops, sent it arcing across the room into the recycle bin. "For them to be effective, they need to band together, which would be bad news for us while increasing their safety. Eventually they'll try something new, but I don't think it will be the clock."

Apparently unable to sit still, Solace got up again—this time to stand behind Tanner's chair. Reaching her arms around his shoulders she snuggled against him. "Maybe we need a power-nap to get the creative juices flowing so we can figure out where they might strike next."

"Oh flippin' pod monkeys," Port hooted. "That is the worst excuse you've come up with yet for a little alone time with your man."

Solace glanced up from nuzzling Tanners neck. "Speaking of alone time, I wonder how Bliss is doing with Nathaniel. I hope she's not disappointed after she has a chance to get to know him on a personal level. She seemed pretty head-in-the-clouds when she left here this morning, and still hanging onto her superhero Bat-dude illusion."

"Bat-dude?" Tanner queried, with a raised brow.

"I'll explain later," Solace promised.

"If Nate gets along with Noodge," Port speculated, "he'll pass the test—regardless of any other short comings."

Solace murmured in agreement then nibbled Tanner's right ear.

"Holy Carina. Get out of here you two," Port ordered, waving one hand as if shooing away gnats. "A single girl can only take so much. I'll hold down the fort and check for updates on the computer. You go play."

Tanner and Solace nearly tripped one another heading for the door.

"Thanks Port," Solace called on the way out the door. "I owe you one."

"And then some," Port threw back at her.

As she made copies of Oksana's picture to take along tonight, Port stopped and stared down at the little heart-shaped face. So young and fragile. She hoped the other women were strong enough to hold on until they could be found.

****

Jones settled into his favorite chair, one he'd had especially made to fit his lovely reptile body, and although it was barely five o'clock, he swirled the brandy around in the expensive cut-crystal tumbler. Humans lived by such stupid rules. When you needed a drink, time became irrelevant, and he enjoyed breaking the rules, a simple pleasure—fewer of those lately, hey old boy.

Because of his scarred appearance, women feared him in his human form. He could have forced himself on them like Smith had done, but the resulting mess and dead bodies were such a bother. Besides, he had other things to appease his appetites—like money and power and two new drugs he'd coerced out of the lunatic pharmacist under his thumb.

One drug made him money, the other made him happy. They both helped negate the frustration and anger plaguing his life of late. He hated being here. Bound by the earth's gravity, stronger than on his home planet, he felt physically heavy and dragged down. And boredom heightened his aggravation. Their leader hadn't issued any new instructions to be carried out, and his personal long-range plans were at a standstill.

Then to top things off, that meddling Fae and her wooly beast had shown up at the backdoor to his restaurant. What a jolt, illustrating how complacent he'd become. But after he'd gotten over the surprise and anger, he realized how much he'd enjoyed the adrenaline rush. He wanted back in the game. It was personal now, and the Fae were in for a few nasty surprises.

His mouth watered at the memory of the redheaded winged female. Gad it had been a long time since he'd feasted on Fae flesh. A delicacy of the highest order. And what a revelation to discover the Fae counted a Rapran among their ranks. While he, on the other hand, had to make due with conventional weapons and anything he could buy, scrounge, or steal. Such a travesty.

Having to abandon the restaurant and liquidate his business had been colossal bad luck. And that howling Rapran had taken out one of his best bodyguards—perhaps in retrospect a questionable description of the Rep's abilities. No matter. Ventures often failed, change being inevitable.

For a while, he'd begun to think all the good times were in the past. What a load. He sounded like such an old rummy codger. For a Reptile, he wasn't old. He still had many good years ahead, many new memories to make, starting now. Because, instead of doing what he was told, he'd decided to do what he wanted.

So far, he'd manage to salvage his sex-for-hire business, and although not terribly profitable, it continued to be amusing. He enjoyed toying with the humans, living puppets doing whatever he commanded. Those two girls escaping boded ill, however. Such a pity they hadn't both been eaten. He wondered where the police had stashed the little whore who got away. She was a loose end, and now he wondered if the two remaining streetwalkers should join the other group of women.

With a sigh, he rested his drink on the end table and drummed his fingers against the side of the glass. The tapping of his claws against the fine crystal resonated with the dulcet sound of wealth and accomplishment. Once upon a time, he drank out of metal cups—never again.

Everything would be okay. He just needed to relax. Abandoning his drink, he grabbed up the small brass box, and held it close, allowing anticipation to fill his thoughts. The feeling grew as he flipped open the lid and delicately removed a pinch of bright orange crystals. Setting the box aside, he balanced the sparkling promise of a good time on the scales covering the back of his other hand. Then he snorted it up as if it were snuff, mocking the social elite who had always treated his kind so shabbily. Regardless of where one was born, or to where one traveled, Reptiles—in their true beautiful form—were rarely welcomed with open arms into the upper echelons.

Heat gathered at the top of his head, and the sharp quills on the back of his neck quivered and stood on end. Then the ball of fire shot downward—all the way to the tip of his righteous tail. A moment later, a rush of hard pleasure tore a path upward in reverse, leaving him groaning and gasping for air.

The third flash of drug-induced-desire covered him

in an iron blanket, comforting, yet holding him down. He struggled to be free, his mind pummeled by the various emotions streaking through him, each following on the heels of the other. He felt safe, invincible, back in the womb, ready to face death. He was all these things, he was nothing at all. The final stage brought release, in mind and body. Then tranquility washed over him.

He'd named the new drug Zero because it left no hangover, and it could barely be detected in the user. The drug chilled him out, gave him one hell of an orgasm, and made him forget things on Earth weren't going exactly as planned. It wasn't habit forming. At least he'd been promised such.

Zero+, the hybrid he put out on the streets, told another story. Z+ turned out to be highly addictive, and much more mind bending. Here were the big profits, and why the turf war with local drug peddlers had been heating up. No problem really, just a temporary inconvenience and useful hands-on practice for his boys. No one was a match for his Reptile Brigade. Except those three insufferable Fae sisters. Mother Nature seemed to be siding more and more with the Fae, but based on who had recruited him for this takeover, it didn't come as a great surprise. His boss could claim a long list of past transgressions, and several enemies—perhaps even Mother was counted among them?

Visions of Smith deteriorating and dying flashed through his mind. The old serum necessary to make them appear human had destroyed Smith. The formula had been enhanced since then, yet, some damage must have already occurred to his body. Why just the other day, he'd found several bright green scales on the shower floor. Maybe his time was running out too. Another reason to forge ahead with plans of his own— plans that would have the humans eating out of his big clawed hand, and there wouldn't be any self-righteous Fae Warriors around to protect them.

A laugh rumbled in his chest, then sought escape. The booming sound echoed around the room as he reached again for the little brass box.

Chapter Six

The three sisters stared at one another, and although tonight's situation couldn't be more serious, they burst out laughing. Noodge howled, and rolled around on the floor.

"We certainly look the part." Solace spun around on her platform shoes, her mini-skirt flaring out enough to show the aqua bikini underwear she wore beneath the black material.

"I can hardly breathe in this corset," Port wheezed, loosening the laces at the top—yet again. "And these leather short-shorts are hotter than Hades' front porch."

"Now, now," Bliss said, adjusting her skin tight, pink spandex dress. "If you weren't so averse to wearing skirts and dresses you'd be more comfortable."

"She's not being stubborn," Solace said, sticking up for Port, "She's resolute."

"Yeah, and it's hard to strictly uphold one's personal philosophy when you're dressed like a hooker." Port eased down onto a kitchen chair and tugged on thigh high boots. "Love the footwear though."

"I feel sorry for all the women reduced to making a living like this." Bliss secured their particle lasers in her tote bag along with water bottles, some food, a field kit, and the photo of Oksana. Famous for her carry-alls, she usually ended up hauling their assortment of necessities.

"I know what you mean," Solace agreed, adjusting the too tight halter top. "At least, with any luck, tonight we can save Yana and Troika."

"And we need a decent lead as to where they took the other women. What the hector could have happened to them?" Bliss puzzled.

"Whatever the answer is, it can't be good." Port secured her hair in a ponytail, and tucked a red flower behind her left ear.

Solace fastened her bangle earrings, then bent down to pet Noodge. "Why does the critter have a patch of hair missing?"

"My fault. I pulled a little too hard gathering a swatch for Nate for his research. He has an incredible lab. It would blow you away."

"Please tell me it's not in a cavern filled with bats," Port said.

"Hardly. But it is behind a concealed panel in the back hallway."

"Why all the secrecy?" Solace sounded unsure of Nate's trustworthiness.

"He has some one-of-a-kind equipment, things he built himself. Doesn't want the government or anyone to get their hands on it or interrupt his work. Not a fan of the Man.

"He also has a big old chunk of asteroid housed in a glass case. He didn't point it out on the tour so I'm guessing he isn't supposed to have it. You should see the stuff he's invented. He's a regular Rupert Goldstein."

"I think you mean Rube Goldberg," Solace corrected.

"Yeah, he's just like that guy."

"Any question where his loyalties lie?" Port asked.

"You needn't worry on that score. You won't find another Hume on the planet who is so into ET's, outer space, planetary travel or basically anything alien. He's like a kid with all this. And instead of being put-off or freaked out about me being a Fae, he's totally into the reality. Never missed a beat when we discussed everything."

"If you trust him, we will too," Solace promised.

"Speak for yourself," Port contended. "My vote's still out. And as the sun has set, we better hit the road, or in this case the streets."

"You be a good boy while we're gone, sweetie." Bliss gave Noodge a hug, and a small motorcycle tire to chew on. "No more eating furniture. You have your toys to play with."

"We shouldn't take the car to the neighborhood we're heading for," Solace said.

"No," Bliss agreed, "or a taxi. I say we wing it."

Port nodded. "Works for me."

Sparkly tote bag on her shoulder, Bliss led the way to the balcony. They'd all chosen tops leaving wingports available, and holding hands, and standing in a circle, they materialized wings and chanted. "To the power of three, so shall it be."

Laughing they went airborne, spinning and twisting and showing off for one another. Then they settled down to business, and headed toward the seedier part of town.

****

Earlier in the day, they'd received a call from the Boulder PD stating Oksana remembered being allowed to go to a laundromat called *Sit and Spin*. Now spotting the rundown establishment, they set down in the alleyway. A small plane grumbled and growled overhead. They were close to the municipal airport, with empty warehouses dotting the horizon. You couldn't beat this place as a starting point.

"Criminy, look at this joint." Solace took a step backward as if she feared the dirt and grime might leap off the building onto her.

"It's filthier than the loading dock of a trash planet," Port agreed.

Bliss glanced at her sister. "And you would know this because…"

"Don't ask." The tone in Port's voice warded off further questioning as she led them around to the front of the building.

Bliss held back her curiosity, but you could bet your bippy she'd darn well be asking later.

At the street, they halted. A young woman stood alone huddled on the dark corner, the street lamp casting a dirty halo of light around her. She didn't look a day over fifteen Hume years, and by description could very well be Yana. "Let me talk to her," Bliss suggested. "If all three of us approach at once, it might frighten her."

In mutual agreement, Solace and Port hung back, watching for pimps, johns, and Reps.

"Hi," Bliss said. "It's a pretty night, considering."

At the sound of her voice, the girl spun around, one hand clutched at her throat. "I'm not supposed to talk to anyone unless it's business," she said in broken English, eyes wide with fear.

"You can talk to me," Bliss coaxed. "Want some

food," she offered, digging around in her tote for a protein bar.

The girl reached out then hesitated. "No. I shouldn't."

"Why not?"

"They get mad if we break the rules."

"Who gets mad?"

"They are horrible. You don't want to know."

"I'm Bliss. You can at least tell me your name." Slowly reaching out, she eased the food into the girl's jacket pocket. Regardless of who this was, she looked like she needed nourishment.

"My name is…Yana." She said the name as if she hadn't heard the sound of it for an especially long time. "But here they call me Candy."

"Not anymore they won't." Bliss retrieved a photo from her bag. "You know who this is right? It's Oksana."

Yana blanched, and tears sprung to her eyes. "Oh yes, my cousin. She is okay? She is safe?"

The girl's grip on Bliss' right arm showed surprising strength and a spirit and willingness to fight if need be.

"Yes. She's fine." Bliss pried loose the small fingers. "And you will be too."

Yana swiped the tears from her cheeks with the back of one hand. "Nothing will be fine again. Nothing."

"Where is Troika? Your cousin mentioned her too."

Yana let out a startling wail of pain and grief, and tears began to flow again in even greater number.

Bliss took her by the shoulders and gave her a

gentle shake—trying to get her to focus and quiet down. They didn't need to broadcast their presence to the entire neighborhood. "What is it? What happened?"

"Troika is dead. I found her when I came in last night. I was too late, I couldn't help her. Last evening, she felt sick, and against orders she stayed in. Her illness was not so great to make her die. I don't know what happened. I sat on the floor in the moonlight beside her body, and I prayed and cried all night long. When they came with my breakfast rations this morning, they dragged her away with the garbage. She was so young. It was too much for her. Too much for anyone."

Bliss reached out and gave the young woman a physical and psychic hug. Sad as this news was, they needed to get a move on. "I'm sorry. That's truly terrible," she murmured. "But you're still alive. And Oksana will be so happy to see you. Come with me...with us," she added gesturing over her shoulder toward Solace and Port where they waited in the shadows. "These are my sisters. We can keep you safe and make whoever did this pay for being so cruel."

Yana took a step back and studied Bliss from head to toe. In their current outfits, Bliss figured they looked more like the devil's emissaries than avenging messengers. As she waited for the girl to come to terms with her offer and decide what to do, two women came swaggering down the avenue from the opposite direction. They were dressed for business, and looked like they didn't take prisoners. Yana cringed at the sight of them.

"I told you before, this street belongs to me and my girlfriend," the larger of the women declared, eyeing

Yana. "You better shove off."

The second woman pulled a knife, the blade gleaming dully in the glow of the street lamp. Bliss bristled and stood her ground. "No need for violence," she said, putting her arm around Yana's shoulders. "We were just leaving." Being a Fae warrior, she could easily have taken down the two hookers, but they looked old school, and not the type to be involved with the sex-trafficking ring they were investigating. Why cause a scene?

"Make it snappy," the first woman said, poking a finger into Yana's chest. "Like I said before, we don't need no foreign young-bloods around here."

"What do you know about these girls? Who's pimping them out," Bliss demanded.

"You ask a lot of questions," the woman with the knife said. "You a cop, bitch?"

"Hardly. Just settle down," Bliss suggested. She needed to get Yana to safety, and to where she could hopefully identify some of the Reps in Hume form. Seeming a bit more literate than Oksana, she might even be able to lead them to the Rep's hideout. And to Jones.

"I think these two need a lesson in street etiquette," the first woman said, obviously jonesing for a fight.

Solace and Port sauntered out of the shadows and stood at Bliss' side. The hookers reared back then quickly recovered their tough-girl arrogance. "What is this, some kind of freak show?" the bigger woman snarled. "All these young tarts are bad enough, how are we supposed to compete with this kind of circus act?"

"You don't have to compete," Port growled back at her. "You just have to move your ass before I knock you on it." As she spoke, Port grew taller, and Bliss thought she looked about to breakout into warrior mode.

The woman with the knife took a hold of her friend's arm and tugged. "Come on, Big Momma, they ain't worth it. Besides, trouble's comin'. The kind we don't need."

Yana trembled so seriously it set her dangly earrings to tinkling. The two unwelcome hookers faded into the darkness, and the three warriors turned to watch a car ease on down the street. The large black expensive looking vehicle had tinted glass, a convertible top, and somehow a menacing attitude. Were the unknown persons inside looking for a good time or a good fight?

"It's their car," Yana said, barely above a whisper.

"They're the ones who got you into this?" Bliss prodded, for clarification.

Yana nodded, and tried to back away.

"Don't run," Bliss warned, "stay in the alley, we'll protect you. I promise."

As Yana relented and relaxed her stance, Bliss let go of the girl's arm and handed out particle lasers to her sisters. The bracelets on their wrists and forearms converted into body armor, and they grew physically more muscular. Tattoos glowing, they manifested battle wings in unison, and as if choreographed beforehand, Bliss, Port, and Solace formed a shield-wall.

The sound of a moan and a thud filtered over to them. Bliss glanced over her shoulder. Yana had fainted behind a nearby dumpster. Probably for the best. She'd be safe there, and they'd know where to find her when whatever this turned out to be was over.

The car crept closer. The backseat curbside

window lowered with an ominous hum, and the muzzle of a weapon appeared. All three Fae shot straight up in the air, narrowly missing the spate of bullets ricocheting off the brick building which had been at their backs.

Engine still running, the vehicle rolled to a stop and three thugs burst out of the back. Before they could morph into Rep form, the Fae were on them faster than a Centurion water leopard on a fresh kill.

Battle adrenalin racing through her system, all senses on hyper-drive, Bliss zoomed past her enemy, knocking the Glock from his hand. Wings back, she did a mid-air flash move landing in front of the musclebound bullet-head, and with laser pistol holstered, she proceeded to kickbox the snot out of him. She was glad for a chance to use the martial arts training she'd received from Master Abbadon, a Dagda decedent. Not only did her skill set her apart from her sisters, but from every female Fae warrior in Mother's contingency. It also meant this unlucky bastard, didn't have a chance.

Using the get-it-over-and-done-with approach, Port and Solace dispatched their attackers with their weapons, and lasered off their heads. Then they hovered nearby, watching and cheering her on.

The rotten scumbag just kept coming at her. Even in Earth-form, the Reps were tougher than regular Humes, and being a fight to the death, neither could or would let up. He tumbled, rolled, and gained his feet, heading toward Bliss brandishing a broken wine bottle he'd latched onto.

Well no fair. If he was going to use a weapon, the time had come to end this little dance. Her next kick sent his nose slamming up into his brain. He stood for a moment, an odd expression on his face. He was a goner before he hit the ground.

All three dead bodies mutated into Rep form. The horrible stench in the air was wretched enough to gag Crap-eating Megaderms on the backside of Darrius V.

Solace set down beside Bliss. "I'll call Tanner. Hopefully, he can get the Army ET squad here to clean up this mess before any civilians find out."

"I'll check on the girl," Port offered. "What about Troika?"

Bliss shook her head. "She won't be coming, I'll explain later."

Using her handheld, Bliss recorded pictures of the dead Reps. Three more to check off their list. Too bad none of them turned out to be Jones. The one she'd taken down had fallen in front of the car, the fine-tuned engine still purring. She decapitated her enemy, then decided she better turn off the ignition. Before she could follow through with the idea, the motor revved and the vehicle leaped forward bouncing over the dead Rep and sending her diving out of the way as it continued down the street.

"Holy Helios." Solace flash moved over to help her up. "You okay, sis?"

"What's the matter?" Port asked, stepping out of the alleyway, the still unconscious Yana in her arms.

"Dang blast it," Bliss sputtered, struggling to her feet. "Damn, damn, damn. That could be Jones driving away."

She tensed, ready to take flight in pursuit of their enemy when an unholy howl reverberated off the buildings, and a blur of fur and fangs flew past them.

She didn't know how, but Noodge had found them. He may have picked up on her being punched and bruised as she fought. Lately, their psychic connection seemed to be growing stronger, but how had he gotten out of the apartment?

The three sisters stood in open mouthed wonder as Noodge tore down the avenue after the vehicle. Dogs chased cars—Raprans caught them. Noodge leaped on the convertible top and tore it to shreds. The driver swerved back and forth trying to dislodge their glorious beast, but nothing seemed to be working. The car did a one-eighty, and headed back toward them. Noodge's head disappeared through the hole in the roof, and he came back with what appeared to be an arm in his mouth. One scream later, the car plowed headfirst and at top speed, into the side of a brick building. Seconds before impact, Noodge leaped off and trotted over to Bliss. He laid the detached arm at her feet, sat down, and grinned up at her. Yes grinned. He had such an endearing personality.

The three sisters stared down at the severed limb.

"Darn. Look at the skin tone," Port said, shifting the weight of Yana on her shoulder.

"It's dark, very dark," Solace put in, disappointment evident in her voice.

Bliss dematerialized her wings with an audible snap. "That means two things. It isn't Jones, and whoever is behind this is making inroads developing human forms for the Reps. Now when they transform, they can blend more easily into any country or ethnic group.

"A big step toward global infiltration."

Chapter Seven

The next day, they spent the morning regrouping and spreading Saturnalia cream on their bruises. Yana and Oksana had been reunited, and the police were taking statements and the lead on the investigation. At the Green Goddess office, Port and Solace updated all new information and ran their own search on the VIN number of the big black car.

"It's the perfect day for an afternoon swim," Bliss teased, flaunting the fact she'd been given a reprieve from helping with such boring indoor activities.

When Nate called late last night, she couldn't resist his invitation for another outing. And the sisters agreed it would give her another opportunity to feel him out, and to make double sure she could depend on him to watch her back. Besides, she had a severed arm to deliver to Dr. Calhoun. And unless she was terribly mistaken, which she wasn't, they might be hitting the pond for exercise involving more than the backstroke.

"Don't forget your suit," Solace reminded her.

"Not planning on wearing one," she called with a grin on the way out the door.

****

Arriving at the ranch house, she spotted an antique carriage under a nearby tree. The dun mare she'd seen Nate training, now patiently waited in the traces. The cargo area behind the seat held various items including a blanket and huge basket. She hadn't expected a picnic. Tanner and Solace had gone on one. It had worked out okay—in the end. Not the romantic tryst Solace had been hoping for, but she and Tanner had talked and grown closer that day. At least if things didn't go well today, it hadn't been her idea, and there would be food for comfort.

She parked nearby, got out of the car, and with her new woven hemp tote in hand, carefully approached the horse.

"Hi pretty girl," she crooned, stroking the velvety nose. "You going with us today?"

"What a picture the two of you make," Nate said, sauntering down the steps of the house.

Well-worn jeans hugged his body in places she longed to explore, and the dusty blue shirt enhanced his eyes, eyes into whose depths she could easily become lost. Stepping closer, he took her hand and twirled her around as if they were dancing. Her short white dress, gaily printed with summer flowers, flared out as she pirouetted on black high-top boots. Coming to rest against his chest, he encircled her with his arms and brushed a kiss upon her lips, brief yet impassioned.

"You taste like sunshine," he said.

"Being with you does seem to make me hot," she agreed.

He gave a little bark of laughter, and took a step back. "Are you ready to go? Need a pit stop or anything?"

"I'm more than ready, and the carriage is wonderful. Thank you for thinking of it."

"Guess it might sound crazy, you being a space cadet and all, but you seemed like an old fashion girl at heart."

"It's perfect."

Nate reached in the back of the carriage, retrieved his Stetson, and settled it into place.

"Oh, I forgot, I have a hat too. She set her bag aside, and ran to the car to grab the big white floppy brimmed creation she'd garnered at the second hand shop the other day. "Now I'm good to go." He handed her up onto the carriage seat then went around and settled in beside her.

"You didn't bring Noodge," Nate said, clucking the horse into motion.

"Not this time. Tanner, Solace's friend, gifted him with a big soup bone the other day so now they're good buds. And Tanner thought it might be a worthwhile idea to train him to sniff out explosives."

"Always good to be diversified," he agreed.

She sighed and glanced around. "What an idyllic day. Thank you for inviting me out."

Faes loved the forests and horses and being free under the sky. "Don't forget we're still on alert though. Who knows what these Reps will try next?" She added the last as a reminder to herself as well as for Nate.

"About that. I only received a crash course. I guess they assumed because I'm an astrophysicist I would take all the alien invasion and extraterrestrial info they threw at me in stride. I am fascinated, of course, but it's difficult to gear up for battle when you're facing an unknown enemy. At least in my mind they're unknown."

She liked he had already decided he would be in the thick of things.

"How about some insight as to what they're like

from a personal perspective?"

"Okay, sure, no problem. You should never hesitate to ask questions. Or tell me what you want or need."

"I'll remember that." Nate's expression indicated his needs and wants might be of a specific physical nature.

Trying not to follow that path, she refocused her thoughts. "Our enemy is tough and untiring," she began. "In Reptile form, easy to spot, and hard to kill. To Earthlings, they're dinosaurs come to life. Think velociraptor with opposing thumbs and a fondness for weaponry. If they take their serum, they appear as human as you. We try to keep updated photographs of our enemy in both forms, but they blend in easily, and new members pop up fairly routinely."

"About the serum. Can you get any of it? I'd love to analyze a sample."

"As a matter of fact, although I don't have any serum per say, I do have a surprise for you in a cooler back in the car."

"What is it? Where did you get it?" He gently flicked the reins to keep the mare moving.

"Last night, my sisters and I tangled with four invaders."

Concern shown in his eyes.

"We're fine," she reassured. "And they're all dead. The good part is I brought you an arm to play with. It's in human form, and may contain some of the serum they use for transformation."

"Wow. Thank you, this is amazing." Although Nate wore his sexy cowboy hat, she could almost see the wheels of science turning in his head.

As he remained silent, no doubt already running experiments in his mind, she decided to kick back and enjoyed the ride. With the sun filtering through the trees, the carriage wheels creaking, and the clomp-clomping of the horse's hooves, what could be more renewing?

"Why can't you stop the production of the serum?" he asked, apparently finished mulling data. "If it's made here on Earth, it must be a fairly large pharmaceutical undertaking."

"Good question. If it is produced Earth-side, they either have a private lab, or a Big Pharma under their control. The companies could be cooperating willingly, or under duress. There's plenty of money to be made, so it could go either way. Since many of the Big Pharmas already have underground facilities, unknown to the general public, and possibly to the government, their ability to work undetected is already in place."

"Or," Nate speculated, "it could be coming from anywhere in the Universe."

"Worse yet, the Multiverse. And yes, that's a possibility too."

"How about some blood from one of them while they're in Rep form? Maybe we could create a chemical to eliminate them biologically."

"Well there's usually plenty of the green stuff around when we butt heads. I'll be sure to save you some next time we take them down in Rep form."

He glanced at her. "That'd be great. Although, I feel a little guilty hoping you'll run into them again soon."

"Don't worry. It's inevitable."

So far, it sounded like having Nate on their team

would be groundbreaking. But assessing his strengths and weaknesses seemed more complicated than she had anticipated. He'd turned out to be a complex man. Could she trust him with her life? That's what partners did, and if they were going to bring him into the inner circle, they had to be drop-dead sure of his allegiance.

Nate's brainiac ways and equipment were certainly a plus. Mother had supplied them with a dandy little lab next to the office, but its usefulness proved somewhat limited and terribly elemental compared to Nate's setup. Besides, true experimentation generally involved math, which was to be avoided at all cost. On the other hand, while being intrigued by alien species counted on the plus side, what if Nate actually harbored some misplaced sympathy toward the Reps—they were aliens too.

They eased to a halt under a sprawling cottonwood tree, and Bliss' niggling thoughts dissolved away in the face of the beauty before her. On the left, a stream rushed by, the water singing and dancing on its journey from mountain top to parts unknown. Nearby, and sheltered by a stand of Aspen, the water had been diverted with boulders creating a pond, its mirrored surface reflecting beams of sunlight. A wooden dock extended a few feet out onto the shimmering blue disc.

The carriage springs squeaked and dipped when Nate got out. She studied him as he came around to her side. His aura seemed even more pronounced in the out-of-doors. Right now it glowed a rich golden yellow, a sign of an analytical intelligent mind, but also seen in a person successful and happy with their own company. She had to admit, those words summed him up quite nicely.

When he took her hand, she let the color fade away. Being a warrior, trained in several forms of combat, it felt special to be treated like a delicate being. He helped her down, then unhitched the horse, leaving the mare haltered and ground-tied to wander at will. After handing out the picnic basket, he grabbed the blanket, and ushered Bliss closer to the water's edge.

"Swim first or food?" he asked, spreading out the blanket.

"Swim," she decided, setting the basket aside.

He tossed his hat on the blanket, and began unbuttoning his shirt.

She glanced around while removing her hat, then dropped it on the blanket beside his. "Where is Alfonso today?" Although she thought highly of Nate's compadre, his penchant for unexpected arrivals had her concerned.

"No worries. He went to town for supplies, and usually spends the day with his cronies, catching a meal at the VFW and talking about the old days. He also has a senorita there who has captured his heart."

She wondered what it would take to capture Nate's heart. Naked to the waist, he sat on a fallen log and pulled off his boots and socks. Unbuckling her ankle boots, she followed suit. They stood up at the same time and faced one another. Reaching out she undid his belt buckle and carefully eased down the zipper on his jeans. His pants hit the ground, and he stood before her near-naked and glorious. Blue eyes bright as gem stones, his body lithe as a well-muscled jungle cat, his interest obvious based on the bulge beneath the boxers he still wore.

Bliss gathered up the hem of her dress and brought

it up over her head.

"Purple is my favorite color," he said, eyirg her bikini bottom underwear, and what it barely covered.

"Good." She stepped closer until nothing stood between them but scraps of clothing and hot desire. Resting her hands on his chest, she petted the light shadowing of hair, and traced the dips and curves of his muscles. "If we don't go swim now, I doubt we ever will," she whispered against his cheek.

"Would that be so terrible?"

"No. But I've never been kissed underwater. And new things are so exciting." Would he find her confession intriguing?

"Then by all means," he said, without hesitation, "last one in's a rotten ovum."

Before she realized she'd been challenged, he broke away, ran down the dock, and cannonballed into the water.

With a totally un-warrior-like squeal, one she didn't even know she owned, she followed, holding her breath, bracing for a freezing jolt. What a surprise when lukewarm water closed over her, comforting and inviting.

Swimming came as easily to her as flying, both undertakings sharing a similar exhilaration. And although nothing could trump the freedom offered by taking to the air, this came close. She dove deep, sending the small fish scattering in all directions, the light refracting through the water turning them into flashes of silver.

Grabbing a quick breath she shot back down to the bottom of the pool, twisting and pirouetting, sending the tall grasses to waving. She'd forgotten how much fun swimming could be. On Aqueous II, she'd logged hundreds of hours, but for training purposes and it hadn't been fun. She'd sworn if she had to sleep, eat, and drink there one more week, she would have sprouted fins and gills.

Just for a lark, Bliss circled the perimeter three times at top speed, creating a vortex as she stirred the pool like a big earthen pot. Breaking the surface, she laughed with glee as waves and whitecaps crashed around her.

Nate popped up behind her. "Holy cow, I thought a tornado had touched down—but it was just a beautiful Fae." When he nuzzled the nape of her neck, she turned around, playfully aimed a kiss at his mouth, and dove sideways calling, "Catch me if you can."

His growl of laughter grew indistinct as she rocketed through the water using a mermaid kick. Sleek and powerful, she could stay underwater longer then a pearl diver, and with senses on high alert, she became one with the rhythm of the underwater world—one with the little creatures who made their home there.

Diving down just as deep, Nate swam beside her. His lean well-muscled body serving him well underwater. They swam face to face, holding on to one another. Then they hovered suspended, all senses trained on the kiss they now shared. Did the whirring in her ears come from being underwater, or from the excitement racing through her body? Hands touching, fingers interlocked, they slowly rose to the surface, their lips never parting.

Breaking apart, gasping for air, the desire for more kissing and touching overwhelmed Bliss. But she mustn't appear too eager—a girl liked a little courtship.

Pretending to ignore him, she floated on her back, leisurely riffling her hands to keep steady, the water sluicing up and down, over and under, tickling her in the most intimate of places.

Nate dipped under the water, and swam beneath her, the length of his body whispering past hers without touching it. When he came up for air and reached for her she arched backwards, seeking the watery depths. He grabbed at her feet, but she easily broke free, and they chased one another like singing sea otters. Deciding she wanted to be caught, and fearing to injure his male pride if she kept eluding him forever, Bliss headed toward the side of the pond and the slew of boulders cascading from the grassy level into the water.

Gaining shallower ground, they clung to one another, the water lapping at chest level. He turned her around, and gathered her long hair to one side. "I adore your red mane." Standing at her back, he teased kisses along her neck and shoulder.

In spite of the cool water, the heat of passion flared in her belly, and flashes of things to come shot downward making her toes curl in the sand. If only she could stay this way for hours. Yet to be fair, he'd hardly had any fun at all. She turned around to face him, and the heat from his body covered her like a warm caress. When he bumped up against her, she realized his boxer shorts were gone, and somewhere along the way her lavender panties had come off.

"Your Celtic tattoos intrigue me," he whispered, gliding the fingertips of one hand across them. "Are you a beautiful Selkie," he crooned, "come to steal my heart? Or perhaps, you're an Undine. An even more enchanting water nymph."

Gini Rifkin

"They're both overrated," she warned, playfully. "And they're not always faithful where affairs of the heart are concerned. You should stick with the Fae. You're in good hands with the Faerie-folk." For emphasis, she trailed hers downward from his chest to his stomach to his…

Head back, he groaned, encouraging her to keep going. Then suddenly, he gripped her wrist, and led her through the water to the rocky side of the pond. Reaching a flat stone submerged in the water, he sat and urged her to straddle his thighs. The sunlight sparkled and glinted off the beads of water in his hair, and it flashed off the rippling pool in bands so bright they were hard to look upon. She felt surrounded by white light, but the red light of passion infused her body.

He inhaled sharply when she wrapped her hands around him, teasing, stroking, fondling. Watching her face, he sought to please her in kind, and they fed one another's desire, taking each other higher and higher. When both their breathing became ragged and desperate, he gripped her upper arms and drew her forward through the water. "I want all of you, Bliss," he demanded.

She half-climbed half-floated onto his lap, taking him in, and they gasped in unison, as he fully claimed her. Smiling, she braced her feet on the rocks and her hands on his shoulders, and hung on for the ride of her life.

Rising and falling, lost to the near weightless ecstasy, she reveled in the sharing of this moment, this intimate joining of two bodies, two worlds. It filled a space in her heart lying in wait for pure love and acceptance. Being an empath, many had avoided or considered her odd. Something her sisters never knew. She didn't pick up on any of those emotions in Nate. His feelings were fused with the wonderment of a child, and the needs of a man, a gorgeous healthy male driving her wild.

Warmed by the sun, cocooned in the safe womb of the hidden pond, every cell in her body went on hyper-alert, ready to burst with gathering energy. Eyes closed, and floating in mind and body, Nate brought her to the very brink. Then as if reading her mind, he eased off, letting her feel the moment, letting her regroup and catch her breath before sending her back beyond the exosphere. Holding her steady, he took her one last time, deep so deep. Her desire shot straight up off the scales, and this time, gloriously drunk with desire, she rode the crest to the end. As she went over the edge, his groan of release followed her. Then all sound disappeared except the cry of delight on her lips.

****

Bliss collapsed on top of him, and working to catch his breath, Nate marveled at the fact he'd just had sex with the most beautiful woman in this, or any, world.

"That was amazing." He brushed a kiss against the top of her head, and the red hair he loved.

She wiggled her hips, which sent a shock of remembered desire through him, then she snuggled even closer against his chest. He took this to mean she'd had a good time too. In the silent afterglow, he could feel her heart beating too fast. Or was it too fast? He didn't know the normal heart rate of a Fae. There were so many things to learn about her. About all of this unexpected adventure.

Bliss eased upright, her tattoos still glowing, her expression one of dreamy satisfaction. "I quite like aqua-sex. We must do it again sometime."

That sounded hopeful. His previously broken heart mended along one tattered edge, but he quickly checked his emotions. He shouldn't read too much into what they'd just shared. Bliss could have any male entity in the entire Multiverse—it seemed unlikely she would offer him more than passing fun. Would it be enough? He guessed it would have to be. They could keep it casual. There was no need to do something stupid like really falling for her.

She smiled, and stretched her arms over her head. Then with a sweet murmuring sigh, she curled back up against his chest, and that one tiny sound refuted all his mighty arguments for never falling in love again.

He couldn't help it. When he was with a woman, he wanted all, and gave all. Not in a controlling way, he would always want her to do her own thing, fly on her own. Ha, in this case, she could really do just that.

His gaze travelled over the contours of her body. What must she be like when she took to the air? Streaking through the water she'd been fantastic to watch. He thought of his fixed-wing glider, hangered on the other side of the property. He knew what it felt like to soar through the sky, leaving the earth and its problems behind.

Sentimental thoughts battered the iron gate around his heart. He put up reinforcements, but doubted they were strong enough to keep out his warrior woman. There were occasions when he still had a hard time believing any of this was happening. It seemed more like great fiction, which brought *Casablanca,* one of his favorite movies to mind. *Of all the ponds, in all the towns, in all the worlds, she jumped into his.* The analogy made him chuckle, but he couldn't help wishing for a happier ending.

"Let's refuel," he suggested. "Our table awaits."

"Oh, okay." She gave a little jerk as if his words startled her. "Great idea. I'm starving."

He gasped involuntarily as their bodies parted company, and they stood. Wading over to the steps formed of rock, she scrambled up the side of the pond, her tantalizing bare bottom bobbing before him as he took to the stairs behind her.

Nate retrieved his jeans and shrugged into them. Bliss pawed through her large tote, came up with and shimmied into a long sleeveless sundress the color of her now missing lavender panties. The slit in the front, afforded enticing glimpses of her lovely long legs. After adjusting silver bracelets onto both wrists, she gathered her hair and twisted, squeezing out the excess water. Fascinated, he watched while she fluffed and untangled those long burnished locks. The end result added a wild heathen quality to her appearance—she could easily be mistaken for a goddess of the forest.

The mare's sudden snort of alarm interrupted Nate's delight in watching Bliss. Legs braced to run, ears cocked toward the nearby woods, the horse appeared ready to bolt. Not bothering to put on a shirt, he jammed on his Stetson, hurried over, and grabbed her halter. "Easy girl. What's got you spooked?"

"Something's out there," Bliss whispered. "Something big." She faced the wooded area, listening intently, and he swore her ears grew more pointy. Now she scanned the surrounding expanse, eyes greener than spring grass, her gaze minutely focused as if she peered through or beyond something he couldn't see. He didn't question her judgment. In fact, his own intuition suggested someone watched from afar.

He led the mare to the back of the carriage and quickly exchanged the loose fitting halter for a proper bridle. Unearthing his holster he strapped it on, and after checking the load, nestled the colt 45 into place. Next he tugged on well-worn leather work gloves, and coiled up a healthy length of sturdy rope.

"Who do you think it is," he asked, as Bliss came to his side.

"Reps. Two of them. Right now in human form. Let's pretend we don't know they're out there. Maybe see what they're up to."

"Okay."

He led the mare to a tree, tied her to a low branch, and looped the coiled rope over another. Then he escorted Bliss to a nearby table laden with dishes, napkins, and silverware, and held out a chair for her.

"This is so lovely," she said, covering her lap and particle laser with the white linen napkin. "I hope all your work won't be for nothing."

"Actually it's Alfonso who deserves the thanks," he clarified taking the seat across the table from her. "He's a romantic at heart."

"Now I feel guilty for being so glad he'd gone to town. I like him," she added, "but I enjoyed having you all to myself...at least for a little while. Zowns, do you think these lunk heads saw us in the water?"

"If they did, they'll at least die happy."

Before she could reply, two men stepped out of the trees and stood approximately ten yards away, a large swatch of prairie grass the only thing separating them from where they sat.

"Howdy." one of them called, inching closer.

Nate gained his feet. Bliss remained seated. "This is private property," Nate said, "so I have to figure you fellows are a might lost."

The enemy on the left took a step forward then hesitated when Nate rested his right hand on the butt of his pistol.

"Sorry to interrupt your doings," the other one called over to them. "We were…bird watching and surely did get lost." He kept looking around as if assessing the terrain or making sure only the two of them were present.

"You'll want to backtrack and then head west," Nate advised and pointed. "The main road's about five miles that away."

One man raised a hand in thanks, and both faded into the trees.

"They aren't going to leave." she said. "They were just checking us out. Wonder if they know who we are, or if it's coincidence them showing up here."

"The scientist in me doesn't believe in coincidence," he said.

"Me neither. When they return, they'll be in Rep form."

Bliss eased up out of her chair. Nate stood transfixed as she began to morph into warrior mode.

Like liquid silver, the bracelets she wore transformed into armor protection for her hands and forearms. She grew taller, leaner, meaner, her eyes flashing. When her wings materialized he took a step back. They were gleaming metal, appearing deceptively fragile, but the talons along the edges appeared sharp and deadly—dispelling any doubt the wings were made for battle. Giving a few preemptive flaps, she sent up a wave of dust, reminding him of an armed-to-the-teeth Victoria's Secret model. But now was hardly the time for waxing poetic.

Jamming his Stetson on more securely, he retrieved his lariat, grabbed the reins, and leapt onto the mare's back. Riding without a saddle wouldn't have been his first choice, but being the only choice, it'd have to do.

"Easy girl," he murmured, when the mare danced to one side. The little dun, one of his best, would be facing a predator worse than the mountain lion they'd come upon last year. He could only hope she'd muster the same passel of courage today as she did then.

With an ungodly roar, the two Reps charged out of the woods. Their gruesome reality surpassed all the pictures he'd concocted in his mind. The mare snorted, but stood fast. With a war cry making his hair stand on end, Bliss shot straight up into the air.

The Reps split up, heading in opposite directions. Bliss targeted the one on the left. He waited for the one on the right to draw closer. When the behemoth came within range, he fired, unloading his Colt revolver. It barely slowed the monster down. He glanced at the rope he held. It seemed rather fragile defense in the face of what headed his way.

****

Bliss dared to flash-move closer, particle laser blasting away. Taking her Rep by surprise, he roared in anger, the bullets he fired from the Glock pistol narrowly missing her. She hadn't recognized either of the enemy as Jones. But she wouldn't doubt he had a hand in organizing this little soiree.

One close range blast took off the Reps right leg at the knee. He careened into a tree, knocking himself senseless. She lasered his weapon into a harmless patty-melt, then hovered searching for Nate. *Can you say rodeo.* Since he seemed to be holding his own, she watched not wanting to horn in on his kill.

Like a Centaur warrior, he rode the mare as if the two of them were one entity, and with strong thighs gripping his mount he took evasive action. Then he lassoed the attacking Rep around the neck. Knowing what to do, his horse dug in and refused to move. Although hard to tell, due to his green face, the monster appeared to be choking. Dropping his weapon, he clawed at the noose, and running amuck in a panic drew it tighter and tighter.

Playing out more rope, Nate urged his mare out onto the dock. The horse rolled its eyes in fear, but with supreme faith, followed Nate's commands. At the end of the wharf, Nate looped the line around the metal pylon jutted up out of the water. Then he ordered the horse to backup. The action dragged the Rep, still struggling and clawing at his throat, into the pond. The wretch sank like a bar of high grade Osmium. Guess the buggers couldn't swim. Good to know.

She gave Nate a big thumbs up then studied her attacker. When he bashed his head on the tree, he'd fallen backwards and smashed the other side on a large boulder. He appeared dead, and coming back seemed doubtful. Still, always best to follow the rules. For such gruesome beasts, they had rather slender necks. Blasting away, she watched with satisfaction as his detached lopsided head rolled awkwardly off to one side.

Still mounted, Nate urged Molly back to the shelter of the trees. Boy, Nate had totally gone cowboy on the Rep. A thrill shot through her as images replayed in her mind. There was something all alpha and yummy about a man who knew how to handle a horse, a gun, and a woman. Guess Nate was now a triple threat man where her hormones were concerned. Whether wearing a lab coat, a Stetson, or nothing at all, he turned her on.

She went airborne, set down by the carriage, and eighty-sixed her wings. Nate dismounted, and took a moment to stroke the mare.

"Good job, old girl," he said, calming Molly a little more. "You did me proud."

"You were both terrific," she praised, as they moseyed over to join her.

"Shades of my steer roping days," he confessed.

"You are such a man of mystery, Nate Calhoun. Which one is the real you, the brainiac scientist, or the kickass cowboy?"

His expression turned sober as he backed Molly between the carriage shafts, and tightened the traces. "It's a long story."

She checked the safety on her laser pistol, and returned it to her tote. "I've got nothing but time."

He studied her face as if he wondered whether or not to take the chance, step off the cliff, go for broke, and offer her a little piece of his heart and soul. He wasn't sure he could trust her. Guess the feeling kinda worked both ways—but it shouldn't.

"After what we just shared on the battlefield, not to mention in the water, I think it officially sealed the deal as far as us being partners."

The grim line of his mouth softened, and his shoulders relaxed. He'd made a decision. Then his expression darkened. "When I'd just turned thirteen, my parents died in a car accident back in Texas."

Another revelation. He was an orphan—a situation commonly occurring where superheroes were concerned.

"After which" he continued, "I got passed around from foster home to foster home. I played hooky from school every chance I got, ran with a wild bunch, and had absolutely no aspirations or dreams for the future."

He crossed his arms over his chest and remained silent, a faraway look in his eyes.

"Sounds like a pretty rough way to start your teen years," she said, thinking of her own parents and how they had raised her. The Fae lived a long, long time. They were known to spend decades away from home, such as during her training years, but not unlike prides of lions here on Earth, the extended family acted as parents too. On her home planet, or whenever she encountered Fae of her clan, she could always find parental love and support.

"It gets worse," he confessed. "I always loved animals. I couldn't have a dog, but managed to feed the stray ones I came across in back alleys. Guess I kinda felt like a stray myself. A few years later, my buddy and I snuck into the stock show in Dallas, and my whole world changed. I fell in love with horses, felt a special kinship with them. In my mind they represented the code of the old west and the freedom of the open range.

"We wandered through the pens and holding areas, and came across a man beating a mare. She had a foal in the stall with her, and didn't want to leave it to go in the ring for judging. I'd been whipped before and knew how it felt. My friend tried to stop him, and got badly thrashed as well.

"I went a little crazy. I took the whip from the man and nearly beat him to death. He seemed to exemplify all the cruelty I saw in the world. I was charged with a felony, but being a minor, and the wretch I clobbered being a repeat offender, they offered me parole—if they could find a family member to sponsor me.

"They'd been trying to find Uncle Zeb since my folks died, and thank God they finally did. But truth be known, when I came to Colorado, I was a young buck with a huge chip on my shoulder." He gave a snort of laughter and shook his head as if the image now seemed improbable.

"Uncle Zeb, a widower with no kids of his own, took me in. Somehow he pulled-off having my prior records sealed and buried deep so I could have a fresh start. Still, I rebelled against everything every chance I got. He and Alfonso even tried home schooling me because I kept getting suspended on a regular basis. Yet ornery and wild as I was, Uncle Zeb never gave up on me.

"He taught me about the animals at the ranch and in the woods, and about putting in a hard day's work. For a few summers, we even rodeod together, bull riding. Nothing like being thrown and stomped on by fifteen-hundred pounds of horned fury to let you know your place in the universe."

"That's where you got the scar." She rested her hand on his left side.

"Nope. Got that from the craziest goat Uncle Zeb

ever owned. She didn't like having her feet trimmed."

"The goats of Capricorn 12 are as big as your horse."

His eyes widened. "Won't be adding a visit there to my bucket list. Anyway, Uncle Zeb also praised and rewarded me when I occasionally got something right. Being happy at the ranch came easy enough, but I didn't fit in when I went to town. Boulderites are opened minded up to a point, but they can be downright snooty at times."

He reached into the duffle sitting in the back of the carriage and unearthed a box of bullets. Revolver in hand, he emptied and saved the spent brass, and replaced them with live rounds.

"Somehow I graduated high school, and Uncle Zeb paid for college as long as I kept my grades up. When I discovered the world of science, especially physics, I knew I'd found the path I needed to follow. But I still felt torn between two worlds. About halfway through my first master's degree, I figured out I could pretend to be what the real world demanded in order to get along and land a job, and the rest of the time I did what made me happy. It's kind of fun."

"Ha. You didn't fool me," she interrupted. "I knew right away you had a secret superhero dual personality thing going on."

He eased over, and studied her closely. "You did huh? Well I guess that's because you're so special yourself with your own secret identity. I thought you were some highfalutin city gal who liked parties and penthouses, when in reality you're a fightin' little filly who doesn't mind getting down and dirty."

"Down and dirty—and naughty to boot," she

added.

"I especially like the naughty part," he assured.

Holstering the revolver, he slowly ran his hands up and down her bare arms, and by the expression in his eyes, she knew it wouldn't take much to coax that smoldering desire into a full-fledged roaring fire.

"I like that part too. But I'm afraid we better head back to the house. I need to check in, and there's gonna be a cosmic ton of paper work following this unexpected encounter. I need to alert Port and Solace about the Rep attack. It seems they tracked us down," she pointed out. "But to be honest I'm wondering who they were after. It might have had something to do with your position at NIST."

"I think they were hoping for both of us," Nate said. "Regardless, two more bad guys are off the list. Unless you have a different protocol, I can take care of our nasty intruders with a back-hoe. "

"That'd be great. And you'll have plenty of DNA, blood, and other gunk to work with in your majorly amazing lab. Kinda takes the shine off the arm I brought you as a present. Don't forget, it's still on ice in the car."

"A man can never have too many severed arms." He lifted a lock of her hair and intertwined the strands in his fingers. "You really are the best date ever."

Chapter Eight

How could it be past two in the afternoon? Despite the drudgery of paperwork at the Green Goddess office, the morning seemed to have flown by rather quickly.

"I hope Bliss is having fun." Solace yawned and glanced over at Port. "She needed the time to re-energize. I don't think she ever caught up after her empath connection with Oksana."

"A day in the quiet countryside should do the trick," Port agreed.

"Nate's horse ranch sounds amazing. Maybe all of us can spend a day there soon. The stables and horses Mother secured for us are great, but this would be even more like trooping in the old days—laughing and meandering at will, no limit on time or space."

Port checked the clock on the wall. "Speaking of time, I hope she gets back for this afternoon's training session with Noodge. I locked him in her bedroom with water and a bag of chow. He's zoned out after last evening's car chasing escapade and this morning's run with Tanner, so hopefully he's sleeping and not eating her pillows.

"I still can't believe he chewed a hole in the penthouse wall to come and find us last night. I don't think the apartment manager bought the story of the damages being caused by a raucous family of raccoons, but he assured me the construction company would be over tomorrow morning to start repairs. Good thing we had renter's insurance."

"Well, I can't believe once Noodge made it to the balcony he shinnied down a tree to street level. Guess we should add part monkey to his pedigree. And we'd better start locking our sliding glass doors at night. If he could get down, someone could get up."

Port nodded and came to stand beside Solace studying the four Rep photos which had been added to the board, and listed as terminated. "A good night's work," she admitted. "But we don't slack off on security and training. If these Reps worked for Jones, he's really gonna be pissed."

"I agree. The way Jones treated his buddy Smith, he seems like the self-serving, vengeful type."

"He has plenty of reasons to want revenge," Port put in. "Besides taking down his restaurant/money laundering gig, now we screwed up his hookers-for-hire scheme."

"Not to mention what happened to his face from my shootout with the drone. That had to really chap his scaly butt." Solace lasered two more photos onto the board, and shook her head in sorrow. "It's so sad we were too late to help Troika."

"But we rescued Yana." Port smoothed out the rumpled section of newspaper the young woman had been carrying in her pocket. "Pretty smart of her to steal this from Jones' wastebasket to learn more English and maybe figure out where they were being held."

"It was. And she's kindhearted too. Even after all she's been through, she's worried about the other women who seemed to have disappeared. Thinking about them really creeps me out," Solace added, with a shiver. "What could have happened to them? It's pretty mysterious the way they were taken away the second day and never seen again."

"It turns my stomach to imagine what those jaundiced pukes wanted them for."

"Once Bliss gets home," Solace said, calling up a map on the Mother Board, "we need a plan to track down their whereabouts. We must have enough clues to put something together."

"Bliss really likes Dr. Calhoun," Port mused. "Hope he knows if he hurts her, grief will rain down on him so fast and hard it will blow Newton's law of universal gravitation to Helios and back."

"Take it easy, Port. You didn't like Tanner at first either," Solace pointed out. "And now you've been known to actually complement him on occasion. I'm sure Nate will win you over eventually. Let's face it. You just don't like Humes much."

"We'll see. Unlike the two of you, I have no romantic aspirations to skew my objectivity."

"It doesn't hurt to have a little fun along the way. Tanner still makes my knees week and my heart pound." At the thought of him, Solace felt a tingling in some other areas too, areas better left unnamed. "That said, I might have to spend the night at his place."

"See what I mean. Males, regardless of species, complicate everything. You'll be with Tanner, Bliss will be with Nate, and I'll be home babysitting the giant hairball. It sucks," Port groused.

"I think someone is jealous," Solace teased. "And it's your own fault. If you weren't so drop dead determined to mate only with male Faes, you could be getting what you need."

"What I *need* right now," Port declared, "is food, not a roll in the hay or anyplace else. I'm starving."

"Okay," Solace conceded, as she headed toward the kitchenette in the back of their office. "I'll make us a galaxy of snacks and big dippers."

"Great," Port agreed, taking a seat. "I'll check the computer for updates."

When the front door buzzer sounded, Port nearly catapulted out of her chair. Although their agency was simply a cover for their mission, occasionally someone came by, and assuming they were a real business, they rang the dang bell.

Gaining her feet, she crossed the room and opened the door. A deliveryman met her gaze. No one had ordered anything lately, but the little guy appeared legit. He wore those cute shorts and a shirt with a name tag. Even had on a visor hat. He stared up at her face then ogled her from head to toe.

"Knock it off buster," she advised, "or I'll give you a show you'll neither want nor enjoy."

"Yes ma'am." He dropped his gaze and studied the floor. "Sign here, please."

By Mithras, she hated being ma'amed. Trying not to take it personal, she scrawled her name on the little handheld recorder he extended her way then accepted the package he'd brought.

"Have a nice day," he bleated, before beating a hasty retreat.

"Yeah, yeah, you too," she mumbled.

Shutting the door, she inspected the package for a return address. There wasn't any. Better follow protocol on this one.

Holding the parcel gingerly, she crossed the room

and carefully set it on the table. Her stomach growled—no need to roust Solace and take her away from the food prepping. She'd scan the package for explosives. If anything looked suspicious, then she'd give her sister a holler. She'd probably insist on calling the PSBT, but the Public Safety Bomb Technicians always created such a circus, and it usually turned out to be a waste of time. Or maybe Tanner would want to get the Army involved. But she was getting way ahead of herself.

Opening the storage cupboard, she retrieved the new equipment Mother had sent over. The device, a sophisticated high-tech x-ray contraption, offered state of the art sensors which could detect and interpret sounds, odors, and images from various suspicious items.

While the apparatus warmed up, she put on safety glasses and kicked on her own heat seeking ability, zeroing in on the small parcel.

Nothing seemed amiss...BLAM

The blast sent her reeling backward into a file cabinet. A fine mist sprayed into the air around her, and she started to choke.

"Don't come in," she ordered when she heard Solace running from the backroom. "Close the door," the words came out around the hacking cough tearing at her lungs. "Seal off the area," she gasped, "don't you dare come in without a hazmat suit."

Unable to hold on any longer, and praying Solace understood what had happened, she pitched headfirst into a wave of darkness.

****

Bliss burst into the hospital room, Nate at her side. "How is she? What happened? Where's the doctor?"

All Solace had told her on the phone was that Port had been hurt and transported to the Fae Clinic."

Solace grabbed her and ushered her and Nate back out into the hall. "Bliss, settle down. She's stable. At least for now." Solace hugged her close. "I know, I know. I'm scared too."

Bliss pulled away. Both women had tears in their eyes. "Okay, start from the beginning," she demanded.

"A package came special delivery this afternoon," Solace began. "No return address. Port followed protocol and started the scanning procedures. Before she'd hardly begun, there was an explosion, and some kind of bio-agent misted into the air. She couldn't help but inhale it. I tried to help, but she ordered me back, afraid I'd be contaminated too. By the time I suited up and got to her, she was unconscious. Afraid to waste time calling an ambulance, I put her in a suit as well and drove us here."

"Well what in the Multiverse is wrong with her?"

"We don't know. The poison she inhaled isn't registered anywhere. Mother is checking for it off-Earth. Port won't wake up, and her vital signs are only stable now because she's had a unit of my blood. You need to go with the nurse and donate too."

"Yes of course. We can't lose our big sister, Solace. We can't."

"I know. We won't."

"Is it contagious?"

"It's no longer a danger airborne. We aren't sure about bodily fluids. So we need to take precautions, but no strict isolation."

"Any clues who did this?"

"Yes. Tanner sent his men to grill the delivery boy

and the company he worked for. It turns out Jones hired them to make the delivery, they recognized his human form photo. The Fae-eater didn't even bother to disguise himself."

Bliss nodded. "It doesn't bode well. Especially after what happened to us today."

Solace went an even lighter shade of pale. "What are you talking about?"

"Two Reps attacked us at Nate's ranch. But they won't be bothering us or anyone else again. Nate cowboyed-up and between the two of us, they're history."

"Port had been hypothesizing about Jones being on some kind of vendetta to take out the three of us, and it sounds like she could be correct. He's watching us, knew where the two of you were. And Tanner determined the package wasn't on a timer. Jones detonated it—by hand. The equipment wouldn't have had a terribly long range so he had to be nearby, probably watching it all go down. He knew Port had the package in her arms. It could have just as easily been me instead of her. Oh Bliss, I wish it had been me."

"It shouldn't have been any of us. We underestimated Jones."

"Would you trust me with a sample of Portence's blood, and any traces of the poison you may have?" Nate asked.

"It's all right," Bliss reassured, at Solace's silence. "Nate has a PhD in biochemistry, as well as astrophysics, and like I told you guys before, he has a lab which puts anything they have here to shame Do it Solace. It may be our only chance to save Port. I'll be back as soon as they draw my blood."

****

Bliss tried to lie still on the cart as they sucked a couple units of blood out of her. They were only supposed to take one, but she insisted they take two. The way Solace described Port's condition, she would need it, and it would save time in not coming back to do it later.

They were divided again, this time by illness rather than light years. Either way seemed just as hard to bear. Their first separation had been due to a teenage prank involving a unicorn and a Stonehenge Solstice celebration. Mother wasn't big on practical jokes, and as punishment the three sisters had been torn apart for many years, training and working as part of Mother's brigade. Only recently, had they been allowed to catch up on Spacebook. Being back together still felt new and fragile. And while they were thoroughly trained as warriors, they also had the sensitivities of Fae folk, which meant family was everything.

She should have suspected something terrible lay on the horizon. She had been having such a good time with Nate, loved being with her sisters, and felt proud to be on this mission. Then as usual, all her positive energy hit a wall and shattered like spun glass.

Bliss hadn't harbored a fear of happiness until after being separated from her sisters. Port and Solace seemed to have gotten along better in absentia. But her spirit had sadly languished until starting her martial arts training, which had been a spiritual journey as well as a physical learning experience.

Sometimes Bliss thought Mother didn't realize what a psychological wound she had caused by sending them their separate ways. That's the reason why she hadn't pursued a serious relationship with any male on any planet. The thought of falling in love and losing that person terrified her. Just look what had happened to Solace. She had been in love with Duncan since they were children. They grew up together, and everyone thought how lucky the two of them were to be allowed to go off to training at the same time. But then Duncan died. And even though Solace survived his loss, barely, and had met and fallen in love with Tanner, Bliss didn't think she had the same kind of strength or courage. Being a free-spirit, no strings attached, that's what worked for her. Although, at times, Nate had her questioning that philosophy.

It might be nice to have someone in her life to wake up to and care for—besides Noodge.

Chapter Nine

Bliss twitched then jumped to full wakefulness, banging the back of her hand on the nearby bed railing. Sitting up in the chair, she glanced across the room. Solace still slept. They had both given more blood last night and were too tired to drive or even fly home. Besides, they wouldn't have left even if they weren't exhausted. Instead they bedded down on lounge chairs beside Port. The furniture turned out to be hideously uncomfortable, and she hoped the crick in her neck wasn't permanent. But to be honest, she'd slept in worse conditions, and for Port, would endure any pain if it would help.

The special duty nurse glided into the room, her white rubber-soled shoes making soft squeaky noises as she crossed the floor. Eyes at half-mast, Bliss watched the woman monitor the machines hooked up to her sister. Since Port had nearly been murdered right under their noses, they'd run a double security check on the nurse and all the employees. Although Mother had created the Fae Clinic especially for Fae emergencies, but they couldn't be too careful.

After the woman left, she glanced over to her other sister. Had the bio-bomb been intended to kill both Port and Solace? Smarter than most Reps, Jones worked under the radar. A loose cannon, but one that could still fire with deadly accuracy.

By design, Reps were unfeeling tools of destruction—they followed orders, they didn't give them. Jones on the other hand had ambitions beyond his fellow brutes, and he probably had his brothers-in-arm working for him, creating his own band of mercenaries.

"You awake," Solace whispered.

"Yes. The nurse just checked on Port. I don't think there's been any change."

"Zowns, I'm as stiff as this lounge cushion." Solace yawned and stretched.

"Me too," Bliss admitted. "Where do you suppose Jones got the poison?"

"The source is a puzzler. Even Mother hasn't been able to find out. Another well-kept secret, like where they're getting the transformation serum. Or where the women are being kept. It's one dang mystery after another."

Bliss shoved her hand in her tote and groped around hoping to find a comb. Instead, she pulled out the sheet of newspaper Yana had stolen. Poor thing. Sometimes the workings of the Multiverse or the Fates, or whatever you believed in, just seemed downright cruel. For all her good intentions in coming to this country, the young woman had only gotten a tough lesson on the evils and sorrows in the big bad world.

Toying with the tattered paper, she examined it more closely. It bore an impression in the middle, as if the imprint had been created when someone circled something from the previous page. Since this came from Jones' trash, she wondered what he had circled, what had sparked his interest.

"My cell," Solace said, fishing the handheld out of her jeans pocket. "It was on vibrate."

Hoping they had a new clue to follow, Bliss gained her feet, and shrugged into her jacket.

"Okay. We'll give them a little time then follow through." Still talking, Solace stood too, and glanced over at Bliss. "Thanks. Catch you later."

"Who was that?"

"Tanner. The Army E.T. squad located Troika's body in a dumpster not far from the street where we found Yana. I told him we'd give the Boulder PD and the ME time to do their thing then we'd head over and gather any new information."

"This just breaks my heart. We have to be sure she receives a proper burial, either here or in her homeland."

"We will Bliss," Solace promised, giving her a hug.

They stood staring down at Port. Framed by the white linens, with a poison-generated whitish complexion, and her white hair, now blue tinged for some odd reason, she looked like an Ice Princess from the northern frost-fields of Crystalline B. None of them had enjoyed their rotation to that planet. Warrior or otherwise, cold did not a happy Fae make.

"I hate to leave her side," Bliss said. "But I suppose we'll do her more good in the field than just sitting here staring at her."

A tear marked Solace's cheek. "She wouldn't even wake up for a banana Popsicle."

"I'll do another empath connection with her this afternoon," Bliss offered. "When I tried last night, I kept meeting resistance and I had to cut it short. But it seemed to help a little."

"Made you a little sick too though didn't it?"

Solace prodded.

"Not much." Bliss didn't need to be reminded. The shaking and lack of energy had improved with a good meal and herbs, but the pain in her head had only recently subsided. And now, she also battled lack of blood. "We'd better eat hearty while we're out."

"You'll get no argument from me on that score." Solace bent down and kissed Port's cheek.

"Hang in there, Port. We love you."

Bliss did the same. "Come back to us," she whispered in her big sister's ear.

****

Over lunch, Bliss discussed the newspaper article with Solace. "We can pull up a back copy at the office, or maybe track down an original. I keep thinking it's important."

"Good idea. What's Nate up to today?"

"I don't know. Haven't spoken to him since last night when I met him at the apartment and he picked up Noodge. The critter really needed to get out. We're lucky there's a stick of furniture left without chew marks. And thanks," she groused, "for letting him tear up all my pillows."

"Port locked him in your room not me," Solace protested.

"Oh sure. Blame it on Port when she can't defend herself."

"Be sure to thank Nate for taking care of our little Rapran." Solace said, obviously seeking to change the subject.

"I will. I'll drive out there later and check on both of them. Although Nate loves animals, saddling him with Noodge for an extended period of time is asking a lot. Or maybe he'll saddle Noodge. I sure hope he works a miracle in his wonder lab."

"Me too. Things going good with the two of you?"

What could she say? Nate embodied everything she appreciated in a male. Smart and strong, with an alpha streak tempered by a gentleness that sent her heart soaring. "I really like him, Solace. And I'm inspired by your relationship with Tanner. I know your heart broke when Duncan died, yet you were courageous enough to risk loving Tanner. But if I give it my all and things don't work out, there might not be anything left of me."

"But if you don't give it your all and it doesn't work, you'll always wonder if that's why. I know being an empath your feelings run deep. Probably deeper than mine or Port's, and you take after the bohemian side of the family, fancy free and no strings. Still, love with the right person can be magic."

"But how will I know if it's magic or hormones? We're great together, but what if he only likes me because I'm an alien species. I'm glad it doesn't bother him, but he's got me on a pedestal, and it feels pretty darn shaky up there."

"I guess just give it time. Enjoy what he offers and see where it leads. If the magic is there, you'll know. Besides, how many men are going to take such a shine to Noodge? You have to give him kudos for that."

Their waitress brought their check for lunch, and Bliss snatched it up. "I'll pay for all of it," she offered. "My brain is on overload. No way can I do the math to split the bill. You leave the tip." She held the ticket up for Solace to read the total and calculate the amount.

"Okay, I got it.

"Think we've given them enough time to finish at

the morgue?" Bliss counted out the correct amount of money to cover the check. The on-scene forensics work done by the Army E.T. squad offered good solid basic intel, but they needed the full autopsy report.

"Only one way to find out," Solace said, adding the tip and heading for the door.

****

When Smith had been on the rampage and bodies were piling up daily, the Boulder PD had welcomed their assistance with open arms. The department showed equal hospitality today, and hopefully their civilian status consultations wouldn't stir up too much curiosity.

Detective Bannerman cleared them through, issuing temporary passes to the morgue. "There's a second body besides the young woman found in the dumpster," he informed them. "Came in late last night. The ME already has her. A few kids partying in the park found this one."

"Any idea how she died?" Bliss asked.

"No. Not yet. Something strange going on though."

"What makes you think so?" Solace prompted.

"Well for one thing, you two are here."

Perhaps they weren't being as unobtrusive as she thought. Not wishing to be put on the spot to elaborate further, they made a bee-line to the morgue.

****

Entering the land of the dead, Bliss flung up a protective shield of energy.

"Morning," Solace greeted the ME. "Good to see you. Sorry for the circumstances."

Dressed in his long white coat, hands gloved in latex, bone saw in one hand, cup of coffee in the other, the ME gave her a nod.

"Figured you folks would be showing up on this one."

"Thanks, I think," Bliss said. That cinched it. They obviously had a reputation for dabbling in the unusual. "Anything new on the young girl named Troika?"

"Having been chucked into a garbage heap has compromised a lot of the evidence," he stated bluntly, but he took care turning back the white sheet covering her body. For all his bluster you could tell he treated the dead with due respect, and a fleeting shadow of sadness crossed his face as he stared down at the small body dwarfed by the cold steel table.

"The preliminary tox-screen showed she had the same exotic drug in her system that we found in the two Russian women the police now have under wraps. But rather than minuscule, this time the amount was much larger, and could easily have caused an overdose. At this point that would be my initial COD."

"By choice or forced on her?" Solace asked.

"Not sure yet. There are a few bruises on her arms and legs. Not too unusual considering what she'd been through. But no obvious signs of a struggle or defensive wounds. Based on residual stomach content, I'd say it was introduced in the food. Contestant number two, is even more of a mystery."

He covered Troika, and stepped to the next table. Bliss inhaled sharply, and glanced at Solace. White as the sheet covering her body, with blue tinged hair like Port, the woman all but glowed. It had to be the same poison. Bliss silently prayed they would soon find something that would help her sister, and vindicate this poor lady's death.

"What did her tox-screen show?" Solace asked, stepping up for a closer examination.

"We don't have all the results back yet, but she didn't have any of the new drug in her. It's a stumper. Whatever caused this condition, systematically shut down every organ in the body. Then it's almost like the process started to reverse itself, but her heart gave out."

"What's this red dust on her hands and under her fingernails?"

"Yes, I noticed that too. We're working on it, but I have to warn you, the lab's backed up after the mono outbreak at the University. Parents all in a dither demanding their darlings be tested immediately."

"I get it." Bliss said. "No problem. We'll need a sample of the dust, please, as well as blood and tissue from both victims. And paper copies of everything you have so far would be great."

"You got it." The man gave a little nod, and left to put in their request.

Dropping her protective shield, Bliss laid a hand on the woman's forehead. The blast of pain and suffering nearly bowled her over. This person had died only last night, and her confused and frightened spirit lingered, fighting to stay with the body. Bliss knew she would need all her strength later for Port, but she couldn't let this tortured soul wander in darkness. She threw a cyber wall up in front of the entity, similar to slapping an hysterical person, and having gained its attention, she swathed it in love and comfort and sent it on its way. Then, trying not to be obvious, she eased into a meditative state to fortify her own energy.

Solace nudged her breaking the connection. "Come on. Let's go."

How much time had passed? Bliss had no idea, but it must have been considerable as her sister held the paper copies of the autopsy and lab reports.

"We can pick up the physical samples on the way out," Solace added."

Bliss nodded, and they headed for the Green Goddess office.

****

The office felt cold, they'd forgotten to set the thermostat. Cranking it up to high, Bliss tossed her tote on the table, and clicking off her handheld, she stowed it in her pocket. "The doctor says no improvement on Port. But she's holding her own and not backsliding."

"That's better than nothing," Solace pocketed her phone too and closed the front door. "Tanner said the Army guard watching her door just reported in. All is secure and no visitors since we left."

They turned and faced the Mother board. The swirling collage of faces, good and bad, kept growing. Photos of Troika and the Jane Doe had already been added—thank you Mother. The police had shown a photo of the unknown woman in the morgue to Yana. She confirmed it was one of the women who had gone missing shortly after their arrival, but she didn't know her name, or why she would be in such a condition. Bliss' stomach clenched. Were the rest of them being similarly tortured?

When the office phone rang, they both jumped a low gravity mile. Nearly tripping one another, they hurried toward the sound. Solace got there first, and put it on speaker. "Green Goddess Environmental Research Agency. Solace Goodeve speaking."

"Mother, here. Is Bliss with you?"

"Yes, Mother. I'm here too."

"Good. I found a bit of new information regarding the poison used on Portence. The basic formula was being produced off planet and sold on the deep-web. The site has been shut down, but it seems what infected Portence was altered after purchase, making it even more deadly. All of the big Pharmas checked out okay, and believe me I poured on the pressure and called in some cosmic favors."

Mother's involvement in their mission seemed almost a personal vendetta. Not that Bliss minded, but it was curious.

"This leads me to believe," their Matriarch continued, "only one or two individual are responsible. Probably using a personal underground lab. And since Jones has been dabbling in drugs as well as sex trafficking, and the girls you rescued were involved in both, albeit against their will, he's our number one suspect."

At the mention of an underground lab, the bottom dropped out of Bliss' stomach. It couldn't be. Nate was one of the good guys—even with his black cowboy hat. If he was in any way responsible, she'd know…right? They'd had sex, had been intimate. She felt the door to her heart slamming shut. She should have been more careful, taken things more slowly.

"Activity is fairly quiet across the country, in fact, all over the planet, with no similar incidents. So I have to figure this is local mischief."

"How are things on Cronos 12?" Bliss asked. "Any chance the male Fae warriors will be joining us soon?"

"No, the combatants there gained a foothold when a band of mercenaries join in the fray on the other side.

We'll still win, but it will take more time. However, I'm happy to report Portence's contact in Colorado Springs will be available shortly, not that she'd much care at this point. Just letting you know. I'm sorry I can't do more for her. When she's able to be moved, perhaps a transfer to a healing planet would be of use. Although all my warriors are tough and resourceful, she's been tested more than some. We must believe she can survive this adversity like she has so many other times. I'll keep working from this side. Mother out."

The line crackled and went dead. Mother didn't use a phone, and exactly how she communicated with them remained a mystery, and right now the least of their worries. Bliss and Solace stood staring at one another. "That's one of the more personal conversations I've ever had with Mother," Bliss said.

"Me too," Solace agreed. "What was that part about Port being tested more than some?"

"You got me."

"Interesting about the drugs being produced in a private lab though. We were toying with that idea, now we can focus in on it more."

"It isn't Nate," Bliss defended. "He has no motive, and he's rich as Midas. He wouldn't take a bribe." This last bit of information just occurred to her, and came as a relief.

"Take it easy, sis. No one's pointing a finger at Nate."

"I'm sorry. I like him so much, it seems too good to be true, and I keep waiting for something to go wrong."

"We'd be better off if you were waiting for something to go right. How are we going to find a private pharmaceutical lab?"

"Well," Bliss calculated, "buying chemicals and medical equipment would be a lot easier with a pharmaceutical license. We can start by making a list of registered pharmacists. Then we can analyze their financials, see if anything looks off. Better check and see who might have had their license revoked lately too."

"I'm on it, "Solace said, taking a seat in front of the computer.

Chapter Ten

Bliss stood beside Solace, as they stared down at Port, an activity becoming frightfully routine.

The helpless feeling welling up in her chest made it hard to breathe, and the wail of sorrow she held back made it hard to speak.

"She looks worse," Solace said, barely above a whisper.

"Which is why I called the two of you," the chief of staff said, striding into the room. "Another round of blood transfusions may help."

"You go first," Bliss said, "I'll stay here and…ah…read to her."

"Right." Solace gripped Bliss' arm and gave a squeeze of understanding. They both knew a full-blown empath connection might help even more.

"May I speak with you in the hall, doctor?" Solace exited the room, the dedicated man in tow.

Bliss closed the door, and drew the blinds against the final blast of glory from the setting sun. Then she climbed in bed and held Port in her arms. She felt cold as the ice she resembled, and Bliss let the heat leach from her body into her sister.

Gently rocking, she fell under the spell, feeling her mind reaching out to Port's. Then she hit a wall of darkness again, just like the first time she'd tried a connection. What did it mean? They'd been assured

Port's brainwaves were healthy and strong, but Bliss felt as if she kept striking a barrier. Had it been created by the poison, or by Port's own design? Maybe it was connected to the nightmares from which she sometimes suffered? Regardless, come hell or a Proxigean Spring tide, Bliss intended to break through.

Rocking and chanting, she tried all the charms she knew. "Port, you shouldn't be wasting precious energy maintaining this wall. If you're holding back dark dreams, give them over to me. I won't leave you helpless. I'll hide them where only you can find them, and only if you want to. You remember, like I did for Oksana. Trust me, sister mine."

Resolutely, she chipped away, brick by emotional brick. Almost there, just a little more. She strengthened the spell. Port moaned, and Bliss finally broke through the barricade—broke through and tumbled into hell.

Blinding light replaced the darkness, and the scorching heat felt like it fried every cell in her body. She was running, trying to find shade, trying to stay alive.

In her mind she knew it was Port running, Port fighting for her life, but in taking on the nightmare it became her struggle too. Linked to her sister's mind, they became one, and only a snippet of the Fae called Bliss remained objective and safe.

She was on Darrius V, planet of the Crap-eating Megaderms—the trash planet Port had mentioned. Why would she be assigned to such a forsaken hunk of orbiting profanity? Not just the traveling dumpsite for the accumulated trash of the universe, it also attracted creatures most foul who congregated and thrived there.

She ran and ran and ran, until her lungs felt ready

to burst. Stumbling through a quagmire of unspeakable sludge, she crawled into a cement conduit seeking the shade despite the smell being magnified by the confined space. Check your laser. Almost spent. No charger here. At least not in working order. Anger and revenge will keep you alive. It's been three days, with little food, and brackish water.

Oh dearest sister, why were you there?

Betrayed. Can't trust anyone. Won't trust anyone— ever again. The shoulder wound is turning septic. Must get off the planet. It will be night soon. Then the cold will descend, seeping into joints and muscle. It's almost as bad as the heat.

There's a rat, a huge Trojan rat. Grab it, grab it. Don't think about it. Smash it's head on a rock. Skin it, put it in the metal pan, in the sun. It will cook. It will feed me for the day. Gag it down. Need to sleep.

Teeth chattering, Bliss shook with fright from facing the terrifying ordeal. She wanted to break the connection, wanted to run away, wanted the pain and horror to stop. Gather it up, lock it away. Do it for Port. Find all the terrible secrets.

Lies, lies, all lies. Tricked by a handsome face and magic hands. Should have verified. Should have kept my head and not lost my heart. He came from Mystica, the planet of illusion. But she hadn't known that then. He became whatever she imagined him to be.

She loved him—so what if he was only half Fae? But he was only half faithful too. He had no heart of gold, although he seemed fascinated by the shiny mineral. He'd played her for a fool, and headed for Caronium where they had the best gold in the Multiverse. She had been assigned to work with him, had trusted him, trusted Mother. Never again. Never again.

Begging for a decent breath, Bliss fought to distance herself from the dream. She must capture it, not live it. Take control. Be stronger than the dream. She visualized a heavy metal chest with bands of Cryptic steel and a padlock of old—no nice silver box for this one. Open the lid, draw it in. It's so strong, it doesn't want to go.

The Megaderms would be out soon. Could she last another night? The Crap-eaters could smell the shit in your guts before you even pooped it out. But they were dumb, and they were slow. Finish eating the rat, keep moving. Have to make it to the loading dock. Have to find him. Have to make him pay.

Now she knew why Port wanted nothing to do with any male other than a full blooded Fae. But it left her heart and emotions encased in crystal—beautiful but untouchable. Oh Port, I'm trying. The dream is powerful, a part of you now. You hate it, but rely upon it to keep your resolve strong to make sure it never happens again. Give it to me. I promise it will be there if you need it.

Mother, help me. Where are you? Even you can't find me. He's cast a spell. I hear them coming, they're huge, they shake the earth stomping and crashing about. So tired, must run. Take the path through the north dump. The one I discovered yesterday. But the trash transport landing area is wide open, no secure cover. I have to take a chance. Surely the trawler will be back soon. Didn't he think I would last this long?

Both their hearts raced, and their breaths came in matching fits and starts. This was wasting more of

Port's precious energy, not conserving it. Battling the images, brow beating them into submission, Bliss forced them into the box. Just a little more, trust me, trust me, let them go. Port's body went limp, her pulse slowed, and she sighed, deep and slow. Bliss slammed the lid shut and draped it in chains.

"We did it, we did it, we did it," she chanted, hugging Port and rocking back and forth.

With the walls no longer up, Bliss flooded Port with light. She also poked around for more indications of dangerous dreams. One caught her attention, and brought her up short, but the energy showed white. It was a future projection not a past remembrance. Another battle, but one in which Port had the upper hand. It seemed connected to the nightmare, but in a good way, full of positive energy. She had a feeling it portrayed Port whipping the ass of the bastard who put her on the trash planet. Leaving the vision untouched and readily available seemed like a good idea.

Port's body felt warmer, her muscles more relaxed. Bliss loosened her hold and tried to relax too. The session had been brutal—but the battle had been won.

Now time to pay the piper.

Taking a deep breath, she braced for the anticipated wave of grinding fatigue as it washed over her. A black tsunami, it tore her asunder, and eyes wide open, she fought to pull together the shattered pieces of her aura. Step back, watch from a far just like you were taught. The chaos will pass, and order will be restored.

She felt thin as rice paper, buffeted about in a sea of time and space. Giving thanks for her gift of empathy, she reaffirmed her intention to use the power only for good. Pieces of color fell into place, and the universe replenished her spirit, but not the light she had shared.

Sleepy now, and drained of energy, she nestled beside Port, recalling when they were young, and the three sisters slept together suspended in the tree bed.

"Remember with me, Port, how we swayed in the breeze, the fragrance of honeysuckle filling the air around us. We'll be okay," she mumbled, her eyes closing.

****

"Bliss. Wake up."

Solace's voice sounded far away, and Bliss didn't want to wake up. Then her surroundings seeped into her brain. At the hospital, not in the tree-bed. Port needs me. She groaned and fought her way back to the annoying light of the real world. Every bone in her body ached, and the arm wrapped around Port had gone dead from lack of circulation.

By Jupiter she felt terrible, and thought she might puke. Tugging her numb arm from beneath her sister, she struggled to sit up, and with Solace's help managed to get off the bed and stand upright. Then she staggered to the bathroom and vomited.

"Cripes," Solace observed, "I'm not sure which one of you looks worse."

"Please don't tell me that," Bliss said, wiping her face with a damp cloth. "I did all I could for her."

"Come and sit down," Solace ordered. "I'll get you some water. She does appear better. I didn't mean what I said. You just had me worried. I can't deal with both of you looking like you're at death's door."

Bliss plopped down in a chair and grabbed the glass of water Solace offered. The universal elixir of life, she drank it straight down. It helped. At least the room stopped spinning.

"Were you ever assigned to Darrius V?" Bliss asked.

"The trash planet? Heavens no. Why?"

"I rounded up a nightmare haunting Port. Remember how I said the last time I tried to connect she blocked me, and I could feel something negative draining her energy. Well that was it. I didn't mean to meddle, but I had to. She was there, Solace, on Darrius V. And it was terrible. It couldn't have been an assignment. Someone put her there, and she barely made it out alive."

Solace seemed at a loss for words.

While separated, they had obviously lived through different experiences, but Bliss had never been through anything close to this, and hoped she never would. Even seeing it second hand through Port's eyes had been horrifying.

"We'll ask Port about it when she wakes up," Solace said. "If she made it through what you saw, she can make it through this. And she doesn't feel as cold," she added, picking up and holding one of Port's hands. "Your empath connection helped. They'll transfuse my blood soon, and that will help too. We'll double tag-team her."

"I should go donate," Bliss said, feeling too weary to gain her feet.

"No you won't. You need all the blood you've got. I'll be here. You should go check on Nate and Noodge, and get a little rest. Maybe Nate's come up with something helpful. Tanner and his crew are checking out abandoned facilities suitable for either housing the missing women, or for using as a lab to whip up the new drug we've come across."

"Okay. I better fly, though. I'm too tired to drive, but I think I can autopilot it. It's gonna take me a while to recover. I might have to stay the night at Nate's."

"Yes, of course. Be careful. Call me when you land."

As she stumbled her way across the hospital parking lot, Bliss downed another piece of the protein bar she'd brought along in her save-the-day tote. All she could think about was getting airborne, and then being warm and safe in Nate's arms.

Chapter Eleven

Halleluiah…he'd done it. He'd isolated the recombinant bio-agent-sonofabitch sucking the life out of Portence. Thrilled at the discovery, Nate spun around in his lab chair.

Isolating the agent deserved a brief moment of celebration. Then he flat booted the wall, coming to an abrupt halt. Discovering what poison had been added to the original formula was a far cry from a cure.

The properties of the main element were remarkable and definitely out of this world. Not a pure form of bacteria or virus or even a prion—the protein thought to cause mad cow disease. This diabolical combination resulted in something totally new, the likes of which he'd never even dreamed about. Coupled with the additional compound, certainly something equally as sophisticated and cutting edge would be needed to counteract this…this what? He didn't really know what to call his discovery.

Nate keyed the information into the computer. He should store the data under a cryptic nom de plume, or at least not an obvious one. The file *Botflies in pregnant cows.docx* should do the trick. He added the information. It should go unnoticed in his batch of animal husbandry research documents, and sounded disgusting enough to deter anyone on a quick search. He hit save, also sending a copy to the rather bizarre internet address Mother had given him.

He stretched his neck and rotated his shoulders, trying to ease the kinks and stiff muscles. He had to keep going. This was a good start, but there was still a lot to do.

The alarm sounded on the mass spectrometer, and still in his chair, he pushed off and scooted across the floor coming to a well-timed stop in front of the machine. The clothes from all the women, alive or dead, showed evidence of Reptile cells, and not all from the same Reptile.

At least three live and unknown creatures were identified. Then there were the two who had attacked Bliss and him, so that made five, plus the four street-thug Reptiles the sisters had taken down rescuing Yana. So they were up to nine, and adding in the first one Noodge had killed in the alley, that made it an even ten. Quite a little brigade of bad guys. It seemed a bit alarming to think they had run into that many in so short a time. At least seven of the ten were dead, he liked that statistic. But other than documentation, this cornucopia of new data didn't help them a whole lot.

Noodge whined and pressed up against the shatterproof glass of the observation booth separating him from the lab.

"I know, buddy. You probably need to go out. I could use a break myself."

Walking over to the enclosure, he opened the door and joined the critter. The woolly beast had found a place in his heart, and not just because he belonged to Bliss. He loved animals in general, and was beginning to love this one specifically. A few days ago, Noodge had ridden right next to him in the backhoe as they dug a pit and buried the two dead Reps. Then they'd hiked up in the foothills and ate lunch together.

In the last few days, the brief and enjoyable outings had been his few breaks away from the lab. If not for Noodge he wouldn't have taken any downtime, and probably wouldn't have been as productive. Even Alfonso enjoyed having Noodge around, and so far Nate had avoided any questions as to where the critter had come from and what his exact pedigree might be. Alfonso was patient, good at watching and biding time. He'd need an explanation soon, however.

As they left via the lab and wended their way through the house, Noodge streaked past him, howling, and pawing at the front door.

"What's up boy?" Something sure had him concerned.

A loud mysterious thump shook the floorboards of the porch. His own adrenaline pumping, Nate grabbed the nearby rifle with one hand and jerked the door open with the other. Noodge leaped ahead. Bliss leaned against the outside wall, pale as a ghost, wings deployed, but hanging limp. A quick glance around indicated she'd come alone. When she sagged even closer to the floor, he leaned the rifle aside, swept her up into his arms, and carried her into the house, taking care not to step on the tips of her wings. Head down, Noodge whined as he trailed in behind them.

He kicked the door shut, and not sure what to do with her, he turned first one way then the other. If he laid her down would it break her wings?

"Are you hurt? Are you sick?"

Dear Lord, what if she'd contracted her sister's disease.

"Bliss, darlin'. Do something with your wings so I can lay you down."

She remained silent, but her wings turned to smoke. Gently placing her on the couch in front of the fireplace, he knelt at her side, pressing the back of one hand against her brow as he sought the pulse in her wrist with the other. No fever. In fact she felt cold as ice, her pulse weak but steady. These symptoms were too darn close for comfort to those of her sister's.

Grabbing the worn patchwork quilt from the back of the couch, he drew it across her body then lit a fire in the wood stove which vented through the fireplace.

"Bliss, can you hear me?"

A murmur constituted her entire response.

"Come on, little lady, you have to do better than that. Can't help you if I don't know what's wrong."

"Empath connection with Port," she whispered.

He breathed a sigh of relief. When they'd talked the other night, she'd mentioned trying another round of cosmic healing with her sister. Thank goodness her symptoms were not caused by the bio-agent, but she sure appeared sick.

"Must let Solace know I'm here," she muttered, pushing at the quilt.

"I'm on it. You rest. I'll be right back."

He texted Solace on the way to the kitchen. Then he grabbed the container of Alfonso's leftover split pea soup, dumped part of it into a pan, and turned the gas flame on high. Next, he put water in a mug and stuck it in the microwave. When the timer dinged, he grabbed it, nearly burning his hand, and setting it on the counter he threw in a tea bag. Giving the soup a final stir, he turned off the stove, poured the soup in a bowl and set it on a tray beside the tea and spoon.

Placing the food on the end table, he dropped to his knees beside the couch and stroked the tangle of red hair back from Bliss' pale face.

"You should eat something," he said.

"Not hungry."

"Not the point."

"Don't be such a big bully," she weakly protested.

"Try to sit up. I'll put some pillows behind you."

Without comment or complaint she did as he asked, but for a female with a mind of her own, being compliant wasn't necessarily a good sign. He grabbed the nearby pillows and shoved them behind her. Noodge sat at her side, one huge paw resting on her thigh. Nate settled the tray on her lap.

"Now be a good girl and eat, and when your done I'll give you a present."

"Long time since anyone's called me a girl," she said, with a feeble laugh "What kind of present?" she added reaching for the spoon. "I hope it's not a stuffed jackalope."

He gave a bark of laughter. "Don't worry. No animals were hurt or injured in the making of this gift."

He wanted to ask about Portence, but figured if her condition had markedly changed one way or the other, Bliss would have mentioned it. And maybe not thinking about her sister or the Reps, or anything negative until she had some of her strength back, would serve her best. Seeing her so fragile and frail took him by surprise, and made his heart ache. He'd seen Bliss in full battle mode, recalled her vitality as she swam in the pond. She had great physical and mental strength. It appeared she'd sacrificed a great deal for her sister. It left her vulnerable.

"Thank you," she said, scraping the bottom of the bowl for the last spoonful. "Need to call Solace. Let her know I'm okay."

"She knows. I left her a text," he reminded gaining his feet. Bliss couldn't even remember what he'd already told her. Not a good sign. "Sit tight. I'll be right back."

****

She dropped the spoon in the bowl, and reached over to scratch Noodge's head. He watched her with adoring eyes, his tongue lolling out to one side. It made her happy the Rapran felt at home with Nate. She depended on her Hume more and more, seeking him for shelter of mind and body. Because of his feelings for her, he unknowingly poured his strength into her. She must be careful not to uptake more than he innocently intended to give. Wouldn't want to make him weak.

With a sigh of exhaustion and relief, she gave herself over to fanciful thinking, and a soft snippet of laughter. For one fleeting moment, when he said he'd a present for her, she'd hoped he meant something really personal like what he kept in his pants. When they'd been together in the pond it had been an exhilarating experience, one she'd like to repeat. She'd surrendered to him, at least her body. Was she ready now to give her heart as well?

She believed in the magic Solace mentioned, probably more so than either Port or Solace. Yet she continued holding back, being a silly baby Morovian goose-chick, afraid to risk all. Solace said she'd know if it was right—know if she could trust Nate with her heart. There would be a sign.

Nate returned, a flat package in his hand. As he sauntered closer, she noticed his attire included another of those sexy shirts she liked, the kind with the band collar. Off-white, it resembled homespun linen, conjuring thoughts of spinning wheels and her Fae grandmother—that beautiful thought was comfort food for her soul.

Perching on the arm of the sofa near her shoulder, he held out the parcel. She clapped her hands, excited as a child, not recalling the last time someone had given her a present for no apparent reason. The wrap-job appeared as if it had been done by the man and not the scientist, it was rumpled with no square corners at all.

Grabbing it from his hands, she loosened the tape and tore at the paper, revealing a matted and framed photo. Knowing Nate's penchant for all things extraterrestrial, the deep space subject didn't come as a big surprise. She studied the arrangement of stars and planets trying to determine what sector it might be. Then she recognized the configuration, and her heart welled with happiness.

"Dead center is Kepler 186f," he said, "your home planet. I thought you might be missing it, and this way at least you can look at it."

Tears misted her eyes and threatened to fall, and not just because she had been a bit homesick lately, but because his thoughtfulness took her by surprise. "It's wonderful. How did you manage to capture this picture? Don't tell me you've stolen the plans for the Great Magellan telescope, and set one up in the north forty."

"Sounds tempting," he admitted. "But no. I have friends at NASA."

She snuggled closer, and placed one hand on his thigh. "Thank you from the bottom of my heart. I'll treasure it always."

"I guess for you always is a long, long time."

"Yes," she admitted, glancing up at him. "My Fae life span is greater than yours. Does that bother you? Create a problem between us."

"No. I could live with that. Pun intended. I'll take, be glad for, and enjoy whatever time you'll agree to spend with me, Bliss. Even," he added, "just the next few hours."

She tightened her grip on his thigh. "Especially the next few hours."

"Sure you're up for such strenuous activity."

"I'm afraid you might have to do most of the work."

"A hardship gladly borne."

"Oh brother. Stop talking and start working."

He stood up, drew back the quilt, and stretched his long lanky body next to hers.

"Wait a minute. Where is Alfonso? I don't want to shock him, and ruin the nice image he seems to have of me."

"He's visiting friends who live in a tipi out on the property. They've known one another for years. If he isn't home by now, he's spending the night. And I hope you are too."

They kissed long and slow, and a murmur of contentment escaped her. Noodge growled, grabbed Nate's left booted foot, and with one quick tug, yanked him onto the floor.

"It's okay, boy," Bliss reassured. "We're just playing."

"I intend to do more than play," Nate said, struggling to sit up. "How about I put him on the enclosed porch out back."

"If he'll go with you, it might be for the best."

"Come on Noodge. I've got another big Rep bone in the freezer for you to gnaw on."

Noodge bounded after Nate. Sitting up, Bliss swung her legs off the couch. The wooziness returned, but not nearly as bad. Gulping down the rest of the tea, she decided the floor would be the safest place for her.

Sliding off the couch, and dragging along a pillow and the quilt, she crawled over to the big fluffy white rug in front of the woodstove. Picking up one corner, she checked to make sure it was fake fur and not some poor dead polar bear. Satisfied, she stripped off all clothing and curled up under the quilt to await Nate's return.

Thoughts of Port interrupted her calm, pricking guilt into life. She should be at the hospital, not laying here anticipating hot sex. But she desperately needed to recharge, and sitting and staring at her sister wouldn't do either of them any good. At least this promised to help one of them.

At the sound of Nate's footsteps, her heartbeat quickened.

"I think he'll be just fine," he said, still out of sight. "He's…" His words were cut short as he spotted her waiting for him.

His gaze never leaving her, he unbuttoned his shirt and tossed it aside. Then leaning against the couch, he pulled off his boots and socks, and shrugged out of his jeans. Naked and unabashed he stared down at her. "Do you have any idea what an incredibly irresistible picture you make with your red mane in contrast to that white fur? You're like a rose in winter." He stretched out at her side. Arm bent, he cradled his head in one hand, the other he slid beneath the coverlet.

Eyes closed, she let him do what he willed. Let him take her away from the heartache over Port, and the frustration over their search for Jones and the other women. She felt so scattered—swirling around in a thousand shreds of self. Being with Nate, someone who cared deeply for her, would help gather the pieces together. But in sharing his warmth and energy, if she lost herself to the moment, she could take too much.

"I should shield you." She mumbled.

Her survival instinct need to re-energize recognized no boundaries regarding the donor being animal, plant, or mineral—all had something to offer.

"What are you talking about?" He leaned back slightly and studied her face.

"Energy can neither be created nor destroyed, only converted to another source. When I use my empath skills my vitality is transformed, taken from me and given to another. Now I must replenish what was lost, and because I gave the energy in good faith, and with a good heart, I'm allowed to receive energy from my surroundings, including you."

He leaned back farther, eyes wide. "Whoa now, wait a minute. Are you some kind of a vampire?"

"Of course not." She weakly shoved at his shoulder. "Well, not exactly. I only take energy.

"And that could hurt me?"

"Make you darn tired. And it's polite to ask first or shield someone." Her voiced dwindled to a whisper. "Don't want to be rude, you know."

"Hush, now," he urged, when she tried to say more. "Take what you need. I'm here for you."

The desire to touch Nate tingled through her, but her arm felt heavy and weak. The comfort food and warm quilt had done her in. Her hand flopped down onto the soft rug, and knowing she was safe, the thought of drifting away became overwhelming. With a sigh she curled onto her side, facing him, wanting to explain more, wanting to study his beautiful face, wanting to make love. The best she could do was murmur, "Thank you."

To be safe, she set up a partial barrier, sort of like turning down her need thermostat. Freely consenting to share his illumination, his essence, was an unselfish act, a great gift.

Closing her eyes, she felt the magic, just like Solace had predicted.

****

Scooting down under the quilt, Nate nestled her against his body. A ripple of heat tripped through him, then he felt an almost magnetic connection to Bliss. Could she hear his heart beating, slamming against his ribs, tripping forward way too fast? The thought of spending time with Bliss had flooded his system with adrenaline and hormones and remembered pleasure. He probably had enough spare vitality to accommodate her energy renewal needs twice over.

Stealing a corner of her pillow, he laid his head next to hers. When she'd needed help, she'd come to him. The thought boggled his mind. He ran his hand up and down her back, as if comforting a child.

Her tattoos twinkled then her breathing deepened and he knew she slept.

Chapter Twelve

Bliss strode into the Green Goddess office, a bounce in her step and Noodge at her side.

"Well good morning, you two." Solace laughed. "Glad you're looking better, Bliss."

"Good morning." Bliss knew she must be beaming like an Opus II ninny goat, and she didn't give a rat's right arm. This morning, after breakfast in bed, and a definitely not tired Nate in bed, she felt on top of the world—in this or any universe. "Any word from the hospital?" she asked, meeting reality head on.

"Yes. I just spoke with her doctor." Turning on the coffee maker, Solace appeared more rested and optimistic too. "And quasi good news for a change."

"Did the updated findings Nate phoned in last night help?"

"I'll say. The Doctor stopped the antibiotics. As Nate suspected they were stressing out Port's system, and not reversing any of her symptoms. In fact, the bio-agent seemed to be feeding on the drugs. She's back to holding her own rather than getting worse, but she's a far cry from recovered. Now they're concentrating on strengthening her immune system. My blood transfusion and your empath connection helped quite a bit, but I don't know how much more her body can take. She's fighting so hard."

There were no words left for how they felt. They'd

used them all. Instead, she just gave her sister a reassuring hug. "How about Mother? Any word from her?"

"No. But Nate sure has come through for us, Bliss."

"Like other parts of his anatomy, his brain is amazing."

"And I'm guessing you're taking full advantage of all those other parts," Solace teased.

"With great pleasure. But seriously, Nate came to my rescue last night on all levels. After having used my empath skills so much lately, I was wasted, and in a blue haze, or a purple funk, or something. You know what I mean?"

"Even with your uncanny ability to screw-up earth colloquialisms, yes, I get the idea."

"He took care of me, Solace, no questions asked. He shared his energy and his spirit. It went beyond simply helping. I felt the magic."

"Well it's about friggin' time. I'm happy for you. If it wasn't so early we could have a margarita to celebrate." Instead, Solace grabbed two mugs from the nearby cupboard, and they waited for the coffee to finish brewing.

Over the past twenty-four hours, Bliss had done a considerable amount of soul-searching. Although she didn't consider Earth her home, coming back here reminded her of the indoctrination years. A time of innocence, a time before the three of them were sent their separate ways. With Port sick, it felt like a separation again, and her emotions had gone into overdrive. Calm and in control, Nate stabilized her. A rock to cling to until the storm passed.

She'd also taken time to meditate as her Dagda master had taught her, which renewed her fighting spirit. She was strong again—just as tough. She was ready to kick some Reptile butt. Which made her hope they located Jones soon, or for that matter any Rep.

"So how about you, sis?" Bliss asked, feeling guilty for thinking only of herself. "Are you okay?"

"I'm great. Tanner came by last evening. We ordered in and pigged out—on food and each other. Right now, he and his band of men are putting out feelers for Jones, and while no luck there yet, they do have a possible lead on a pharmacist working off the grid. We've an idea who he is, but where he is remains a mystery."

Bliss checked-out the Mother board, staring at the new photo. "Out of all the possibles, how'd you narrow it down to him?"

"We questioned a homeless guy hanging out behind the building where you and Noodge first located Jones. He told us the main dish at the restaurant was, and I quote, "*aces high pie and four-of-a-kind cannoli*". In other words, a front for gambling. Not a big surprise as we suspected money laundering or something nefarious.

"We gathered a list of pharmacists, nationwide, showing licensing troubles in the last ten years. But even after checking financials for both the restaurant and the names on the list, nothing stood out. Then, although it seemed too obvious, we ran backgrounds on employees, and one name popped. His files were blocked. Highest security."

"Bet Tanner and Mother took care of that little problem."

"You'd win. This guy started in pre-med. Then got booted out for stealing and experimenting on cadaver parts."

"Zowns, a regular Frankenberry."

"Frankenstein, but you got the idea. After his rejection from University, our man pursued a pharmaceutical education in Bolivia. He graduated, barely got a license there but never got one in the USA. Undaunted, he practiced anyway with forged papers. Got away with it until two years ago when he turned State's evidence against a large ring of black market prescription drug dealers.

"According to the FBI, he opted for the witness relocation program, and ended up here. His new bio states he goes by the name of Lester Martin. Owns a spell book, and candle type shop, where he professes to be able to cure people from any condition, A to Z, with questionable herbs instead of questionable FDA approved meds."

"So he's still a scam artist, probably even sells fake Faery dust. I hate it when they do that. He shouldn't mess with the Fae."

"Just one more reason to locate and take him down. His shop has been closed for the last few months."

"What about the women?" Taking the cup of coffee Solace offered Bliss sat down at the table. "Are we any closer to finding out where the Reps have them stashed, or why they want them? I don't get it."

"Me neither. And with the passage of every new day, I worry more for what they might be going through."

"What's this?" Bliss picked up a flash drive off the desk.

"Nate messengered it over early this morning."

"It came by messenger…yikes. After what happened with Port that must have been scary."

"It could have been, but Nate texted me a heads-up, and the bomb squad checked it out upon arrival. You just missed Tanner and his boys."

"Nate must have worked on this in the middle of the night, while I was catching up on sleep. And not being sure when I might wakeup or be going home, I guess he wanted you to have it right away. So what's on it? It must be important."

"I was about to find out."

Bliss plugged the drive into the USB port. Solace grabbed the remote, aimed it at the Mother Board, and hit play. The two pieces of equipment were not connected by any obvious means, but somehow it worked.

"Nate Calhoun here. The following are the results of my broad-spectrum particulate isolation study."

Printed data and graphs began to scroll across the screen.

"I love it when he talks scientific," Bliss said, and squirmed. "He's so smart it's frightening—in a good way," she added, enjoying the twinge of remembered desire.

Last night, she lay beside him in bed, listening as he contemplated the theories of quantum physics. And when he hypothesized, it turned her on almost as much as when he began kissing the configuration of various constellations on her belly. They hadn't had much time to carve out special moments like that, or to just sit and stare into one another's eyes, or even watch a sunset. Maybe someday soon, if they could take out the Reps and find those women.

"Out of all the Reptiles and women tested," he continued, *"one of the most remarkable particles I found was beet dust."*

Solace glanced at her. Bliss shrugged. She was just as much in the dark on that one.

"Beet farming factories and storage warehouses were common around here in the late 1800's. There are plenty of abandoned properties still standing which were once used for such venues. Machine oil, common dust, and burlap particles were also present which leads me to favor the factory scenario. You might start investigating those types of buildings. The rest of this file will be text, and should be copied, printed, or just held for backup to mine. Calhoun out.

"Hot-diggety," Solace hooted, reaching for her hand held, "this is great news."

While Solace talked to Tanner, Bliss fed Noodge the cat food they kept at the office.

"Tanner and the boys are on it. They were already in the field and located a few abandon buildings worth scoping out. A few of them fit the bill age-wise for our new information. They're going to do a drive by and let us know.

"In the meantime, I found a copy of the newspaper from last week so we can figure out if the clipping Yana fished out of Jones' trash leads anywhere."

Bliss smoothed out their crumpled clipping, and started comparing it to the complete copy. "This looks interesting," she mused. Before she could say more, or even think what the connection might be, Solace grabbed her phone on the first ring, her conversation short.

"Tape your ankles," her sister declared, heading for the cupboard housing their newly acquired reserve weapons. "We're going in."

"Going in where, and what about Noodge?" Bliss asked, helping to pack the canvas duffle.

"I'll fill you in on the way," Solace said, "and we need to get there now, which means flying. So Noodge is out. I wonder if there are any flying Raprans."

Good grief. Noodge could be a handful on solid ground. Bliss reeled at the thought of him flying. Making sure he had water and a toy, they locked up the office, and Bliss prayed when she got back, the walls wouldn't resemble those in the apartment through which he'd chewed.

****

Armed to the teeth, they furled their wings and landed beside Tanner. He and his men were dressed in camo, nearly invisible in the overgrown landscape, but Solace's special connection to Tanner led them to the right place.

"Are you sure this is correct?" Solace asked.

"Checkout the upstairs window. The one with the security bars."

Bliss did more than look. Sprouting utility wings, she leaped in the air, and leveled off on this side of the glass. A bedraggled woman wearing a hospital gown, made a lame attempt to claw at the window from the inside. She appeared weak, in fact quite ill, exhibiting the same ghostly pallor as Portence. Bliss shielded her eyes, trying to see farther back into the room. Only a wavering shadow against a blank wall met her scrutiny.

"We're here to help," Bliss mouthed the words, and gave her a thumbs up sign.

The woman stared back unblinking. Glassy-eyed and weaving about, she didn't seem to understand, and appeared barely able to stay on her feet.

Angered and heartbroken by the image, Bliss drifted back down to the ground

"By the gods," she blurted, surprising herself with such heavy-duty swearing. "I could only see the woman by the window, but I think there are other Humes in there."

"Okay. Take it easy Bliss," Solace said, patting her shoulder.

"These must be the missing women." She absorbed her wings. "What are we waiting for? They're being held by whoever detonated that bomb and made Port sick."

"The place is built like a fort," Tanner pointed out. "And the recent addition of security bars is an added hindrance. Storming the place will be noisy and could take a while. Other than the female subjects, I wish we had a better idea of who's in there and if they're armed. They could panic and kill the women before we can stop them."

"If we got someone inside to reconnoiter, it would turn things in our favor," Bliss suggested.

"What do you have in mind?" Solace asked. Bliss didn't miss the concern in her voice.

"Nothing elaborate. Just the old, I ran out of gas routine."

"Sounds a bit farfetched in this neighborhood," Solace countered, glancing around at the deserted backstreets and dust strewn alleyways. "Who would dare come here low on gas?"

Bliss undid two buttons on her blouse revealing a

hint of lacy black bra, and a good deal of cleavage. "I doubt it will be the first thing crossing their minds." She rechecked the power load on her particle laser, and secured it in the waistband of her jeans at the small of her back. "If Jones is in there, he's mine. He poisoned Port, and sent those two goons to kill me and Nate. I owe him."

"We all want Jones to pay," Solace warned. "You need to concentrate on justice, not revenge. It's bad karma."

Solace might be correct, but Jones had made it personal. Jones had changed the rules. "Can't help it." she said, not backing down. "Payback's a bastard."

Tanner gave her an odd look, and opened his mouth to speak, but before he could say anything, Solace stepped up and placed one hand on his chest. "Where are your men deployed?"

"One platoon is down in Colorado Springs. They've had two minor incidents in the past few days. Incidents reeking of lizard. The other men are watching the secondary sites we came up with today, all of which might contain beet dust."

"Can we have them hold and standby? With the three of us and your perimeter snipers, it might be safer for the women if we ease on in and TCB on our own."

"You got it," he agreed.

Bliss slipped on her Fae bling/armor, and placed her hands on Solace's shoulders. Face to face they renewed and strengthened their connection.

"Give me a few minutes to assess the situation," Bliss said. "You'll know if I'm in trouble."

Not waiting for confirmation, she turned and headed for the front door of the huge brick building.

Deciding against knocking, she tried the knob, surprised when it turned in her hand. Easing open the heavy portal, she gritted her teeth at the resulting squawk, squawk, groan. The grating noise echoed off the interior walls, and dwindled into an oppressive silence. A large conveyor belt, draped in cobwebs, stood off to the left. Bare lightbulbs hung down from the ceiling between the crosshatch of air ducts.

When taking their medication, the Reps didn't stink, but she sniffed the air anyway. The smell of sugar beet dust, encrusting the equipment and hiding in dark corners, overpowered any other scent. A maze of metal scaffolding lined the entire right side of the room, which she cautiously approached praying the staircase tucked in the middle led to the upper floors and the women she sought.

"What you doin' there, girly?"

Bliss spun around to face the man who'd spoken. Old, stooped, and grisly, he didn't look like a Rep in Hume form. Setting free her ability to compel, she ambled closer to him.

"Hi. I ran out of gas, and my cell phone went dead, so I was hoping someone here might be able to help me."

"You need to get out of here," he croaked with conviction, as he studied her with rheumy eyes.

He smelled of booze, and appeared to be a watchman of sorts, paid by the pint.

"Who else is here?" She felt his resistance fading as he hemmed and hawed before answering.

"There's the doctor and them ruffians, for starters," he said.

A doctor. That came as a surprise. Maybe their

pharmacist had fallen back on old aspirations, elevating his status to doctor.

"And the women?" she prodded.

His unshaven face sagged a little more, and he shook his head. "I ain't got nothin' to do with them, but for taking up their food. They don't eat much though. And two of them died, don't you know. One's buried out back. I tried to call the police, but them big fellers caught me and said they'd torture the ones that's left if I ever tried it again."

She had a bad feeling who the "big fellers" were.

"Is the room where they keep the women locked?"

"Sure enough. But they give me a key." He tugged on the chain around his scrawny neck, and retrieved the object hidden beneath his tattered shirt. Then he held the key out like a child proud of having been given such a responsibility.

Then his gaze tracked past her, deeper into the room, and his eyes widened in fear. She snatched the key from his hand and tucked it away, ignoring his yelp of pain as the chain broke. As she turned and crouched in a defensive stance, the old man fled out the front door, and three forms lumbered out of the shadows. She didn't need to smell them to know they were Reps.

Eyes glowing red, they transformed, growing larger and more hideous, shedding their clothing like reptile skin no longer needed. Liberating her particle laser, she did a tuck and roll to one side, and mentally called out to Solace. Shots rang out, bullets heading her way, as she dove behind a large silo-shaped metal structure.

Side by side, as if they'd done it one hundred times before, Solace and Tanner bolted through the door.

Solace went right, Tanner went left. Firing several rounds, they gained the attention of the Reps pinning her down.

Using pieces of equipment for cover, Bliss zigzagged her way closer to the stairs. In their burly Rep form, their enemy couldn't hide as well, conversely they were more able to take a laser blast or bullet and keep going.

Concentrating on the main objective of rescuing the women, Bliss activated a pair of service wings, and hoping surprise would keep her safe, she shot upward to the ceiling before flash moving to the landing at the top of the stairs.

Wings folded, she darted down a hallway cluttered with junk, but thankfully no Reps. Judging by the architecture, she calculated the room and window she'd seen from the outside were off to the left at the end of the passageway. Heading in that direction, she passed a set of swinging doors. They flew open, and she stumbled sideways. The rough metal edging on one panel clipped her wrist, numbing her hand. Pain shot up her arm, and her particle laser clattered to the ground as a large scaly Rep appeared before her.

"Where are the women?" she demanded. "Why are they here?"

"None of your business, bitch. You're too late to save them now anyway." With a guttural sound, he kicked her laser farther aside. "You'd do better to worry about yourself."

Unarmed, and taking him at his word, she backed away, glancing around for something to use as a weapon. Spotting a long metal pipe, she scooped it up off the floor. Although heavier than her six-foot staff, it felt reassuring in her hands. As her Dagda training kicked in, knowledge and experience took over, and the Rep's hesitation sealed the deal.

She twirled the staff with blinding speed, pulled off two aerial cartwheels, and came to a halt with the jagged end of the staff pointed directly at the hollow in his throat. He blinked, roared, and died as she shoved the pipe through his neck. Green blood spurted. She leaped out of the way trying to save her outfit—she'd yet to find anything successful at removing green Rep blood from her clothes. A well placed roundhouse kick sent the lifeless body tumbling sideways like a slab of granite. Retrieving her particle laser, she blasted away. "No second chances, lizard breath."

A shooting war still echoed upward from downstairs, but going back wasn't an option, the women came first. She reached for the key she'd tucked away in her bra, and then hesitated. What was going on in the room where this guy had come from? Were there more Reps in there, or possibly some of the women? Deciding a quick detour might be beneficial in the long run, she stepped over the still shuddering mass of green flesh, and burst through the swinging doors.

Chapter Thirteen

Even the use of bleach and antiseptics couldn't mask the smell of death.

Fighting the urge to gag, Bliss assessed the room. It resembled a hospital lab, or a morgue, and she ought to know having been in both lately. A large glass-front refrigeration unit caught her attention. Filled with test tubes, it reminded her of the one in Nate's setup, but this heap appeared secondhand, and hummed and whirred as if on its last legs. Drawing closer, she discovered the tubes inside held red blood—each dated sequentially beginning about the time they figured the women went missing. There were no names on the tubes, only numbers.

Frick…they were experimenting on them. The idea settled like a rock in her stomach. Were they trying to create female Reps? Or worse yet, breed male Reps with Hume females. At the very idea she felt like puking up said rock. The watchman claimed two women had died here. Maybe they'd been given the bio-agent.

A clatter of noise had her hurrying across the room to a partially open door. Inside, a man in a hazmat suit was alternately packing boxes and shoving documents into a shredder.

"Lester Martin, I presume. Or do you go by Dr. Death now?"

The man turned slowly, one hand on his chest as if to calm his heart. He eyed the laser pistol trained on that precise area of his anatomy.

She itched to pull the trigger, but what if she were killing off Port's only chance for a full recovery. "Hands up, and step away from the equipment— including the shredder."

"You're one of them." The facemask on his helmet muffled his words, but the suit did not disguise his rail-thin form hunched like a vulture searching for prey. "What I wouldn't give to have you on my table." He rubbed his gloved hands together as if savoring the thought. "Working with these human females has been less than gratifying."

He nodded over his shoulder, and her gaze travelled past him to an even smaller room. A female body lay motionless on a raised table, her skin the same color as the white porcelain top. Bliss took a step forward.

"Don't bother. She's dead." Anger and disgust rode his words, not pity. "I don't know how he expects me to work under these conditions. But it has been entertaining."

"Well, playtime is over," Bliss advised, clicking her particle laser up one notch from stun to this is gonna hurt. "Have you got a cure for what's killing my sister?" She drew on her powers to compel, but his ego and need to talk about his work made it unnecessary.

"Close, but not yet. And I'm afraid it's the key to his world take-over plan."

"You mean Jones?"

"Yes of course." She could see the self-righteous smile even through his safety gear. "He's led you and your kind a merry chase, hasn't he? For a scaly brute hiding in high-end clothing, he shows moments of devious genius, especially where survival is concerned."

"So what's the plan?" Getting more pissed off by the moment she clicked the laser up from gonna hurt to fry your ass.

"Oh come now. You won't fire that off in here," he chided. "You'd run the risk of setting the organism free."

She glanced around, and the hair on the nape of her neck stood on end. It might already be floating around the room. The sooner she got out of here the better. Relaxing her stance, she narrowed her gaze, and switching to psychological warfare, she powered up and mentally bid him to speak.

"I suppose it wouldn't hurt to tell you," he relented. "I was searching for employment of an independent nature. I missed the work you see, and have years' worth of experiments waiting to be realized.

"More like your experimenting will have people realizing they've reached the end of their years."

"They're heroes. They all died for science, for the good of mankind. It's an honor."

"If you don't get to the point, you're going to have the honor of joining them." Compelling egocentric blabber-pants people could be sooo annoying.

"Besides working on my research," he rattled on, "I also enjoy gambling. Unfortunately I'm not good at it. But becoming indebted to Jones for my habit turned out to be a match made...well not in Heaven obviously...but definitely off planet. I offered my services in lieu of money, and he gave me the biomaterial he'd gotten through friends on his home planet. I couldn't help but tweak it a bit, creating the deadly agent he so enjoyed using on your sister."

Her finger twitched, but again she controlled the urge to squeeze the trigger.

"Now, he wants a cure. Not for her obviously, but for we humans. The idea being, he could turn the strain loose in the world, vaccinate enough humans to keep as slaves, and have all the rest, including the Fae, die off. It's a rare organism to affect both humans and Fae. Most diseases are species specific."

Holy craptoid, this plan went beyond their imagining. Jones had graduated from infiltrating locally, to visions of global domination.

"Where is Jones?"

Dr. Death shrugged. "Haven't seen him in quite a while. He phones his orders in now."

"Is this the only place where the bio-agent is being stored?" A shiver went through her as she glanced around. She really needed to get out of this room.

"As far as I know."

"How many women are left, and are they all here?"

"Only three of the females remain. Annoyingly, it kills off humans much faster than Fae."

Annoyingly. Not unfortunately or sadly, just annoyingly. This man proved to be as big a monster as the Reps.

"Start moving." She waved the tip of her particle laser indicating he should head for the door. "And I *will* use this. Probably tear a big old hole in your high-tech rompers. I don't think you want to die white as a sheet and wasting away."

He didn't hesitate long before complying.

"Don't trip on your buddy out there," she added

Once they were in the hall, with the swinging doors closed and secured, she ripped the headgear off Martin. No reason he shouldn't smell the putrid odor roiling off the dead Rep.

The man choked and coughed, and staggered to one side.

Keeping an eye on Dr. Death, she marched him back the way she'd come and glanced over the rail leading to the ground floor. The sound of fighting had stopped, and based on the nose-numbing pall wafting upward she'd say the good guys won. Who would have thought Rep stink would be lighter than air.

A moment later, Solace and Tanner scrambled up the rusted metal stairs, heading in her direction. "Will you see to him?" she asked the ex-Ranger. "The women are just down the hall. What's left of them. They might be frightened by you, Tanner." She didn't add, *and if they're infected and you get it, you're sure to die.* "I thought Solace and I should go in alone."

He nodded in agreement, and easily took command of their prisoner.

"Get him and you out of here," Bliss ordered. "The organism making Port sick is in that room." She nodded over her shoulder. "We need the hazmat boys here to contain and control. And get all his notes. Maybe Nate can use them to get a handle on some kind of antidote.

Tanner tore off the rest of Lester Martin's protective clothes. "If anybody deserves to get this disease, it's you," he growled.

Shaking in his boots, and offering no resistance, the merciless Hume stumbled down the stairs, Tanner on his tail.

"Martin hasn't found a cure yet," Bliss told Solace as they headed for the women. "And it's even more deadly for Humes than Fae, which is why there are only three women left. He's been experimenting on them—unsuccessfully."

She unlocked and eased open the door, inciting a crescendo of moans and screams from the women inside. "It's okay. We're here to help. He won't hurt you anymore."

The barren room, cold and dismal, offered three beds with sagging mattresses and filthy sheets. The woman she'd seen from outside now stood with her back to the window brandishing a broom, her will to live still evident in the ghostly shell of a body. A second woman lay whimpering on one of the beds, a third stood guard over her clutching a wet cloth as if she'd been trying to ease the other's fever. Barefoot, their hair matted and tangled, they wore flimsy hospital gowns, their wide-eyed gazes darting toward the door like trapped and frightened animals.

Solace called the special Fae clinic on her handheld, requesting a hazmat equipped ambulance. Bliss glanced around for blankets or anything clean to cover their shivering bodies. Not finding anything, she fell back on her empath skills, covering them instead with a soft pink light, giving them strength and comfort the only way she knew how.

"We shouldn't get too close." Solace reminded, resting a hand on Bliss' arm, as if to hold her back.

"I know. But they're so weak. They're dying right before our eyes."

"At least we've found them. What about Jones? Did Martin spill any info on him?"

"He admitted Jones is the leader, but it sounds as if he's yanking everybody's chain from afar."

****

"Settle down," Jones ordered. "You'll be paid in full, plus a bonus for calling to let me know. The cash will be in the P.O. box tomorrow."

As the lies flowed easily past his human-like teeth, anger made his eyes flash red. He hung up, and threw the burner phone across the room. It hit the wall, pieces flying off in all directions. Although hiring the old alcoholic to watch the lab had been a good idea, he couldn't be trusted. With a little liquid coercion he'd spill the phone number. Besides, now he had no reason to keep in contact with the man or with the lab or with that idiot Martin.

Another failed plan.

He felt like ripping out what little hair he had left. They would have to begin again, not an easy task as the freakishly efficient Fae were killing off Reptile soldiers quicker than he could recruit them to his personal army. And scuttlebutt had it their Rep leader would be Earth-side soon.

At least they hadn't located his newest base of operations—yet. But it would only be a matter of time. Getting off the grid entirely sounded like a good idea. Why not go all out, even go AWOL, and see what happened.

The poison, originally so hard to obtain and now gone, had been a decidedly good plan—well-conceived, but poorly executed. No use going that route again. The one Fae he'd used it on could be terminated by other means, as could the other two winged furies. In the meantime, he had plans to relocate to someplace warm.

He hated it here, even if he were sitting pretty and living the high life.

And speaking of being high… He grabbed his pipe and lit up. The smoke he inhaled sent the Zero sliding through his body, the rush leaving his mind floating and his body relaxed. This method left him more tranquil than when he snorted the pretty orange crystals, and lasted longer. Fortunately, he had a good supply in reserve, enough to keep him happy until he found a new apothecary lackey to add to his ranks.

Clutching a scotch on the rocks in the other hand, he stood before the floor to ceiling windows, and surveyed the countryside. Just for the hell of it, he morphed into Reptile mode, and roared with laughter. With a new strategy, if he could stay hidden for a while longer, things might work out to his advantage.

As he stood there on the brink of either triumph or tragedy, his old buddy Smith came to mind again. Although they'd been adversaries, he missed having someone of his own species and nearly his own intelligence, with whom to spar. Whoever thought he'd be wishing for the old days?

He had no confidence in their leader or modern warfare. According to underground information, a large portion of the war chest had been spent on the transformation serum leaving little for equipment or paying the soldiers. Why did they have to blend in anyway? He dreamed of a Reptile army in Reptile form, crushing the humans, turning this planet into chaos. He needed more men.

With a sigh, he took another hit off the pipe. His mind wandered, and a mellow feeling oozed through him. He'd worry about it later.

Chapter Fourteen

"What am I going to do with you, Natty? You keep forgetting to eat." Supper tray in hand, Alfonso stood at the door to the lab.

"Yes, all right, I'm almost done." Head down, Nate tinkered with the new weapon, adjusting the trigger-pull a hair's breadth tighter. "I'm working on something for Bliss. I'll be right out."

"Even where she comes from, they must eat occasionally," he prompted before disappearing from the doorway.

The last time Nate had spoken to Mother Nature, he'd asked for and received permission to inform Alfonso regarding what was going on. Showing no fear and little surprise, his old friend had nodded his head in understanding, stating his spirit guide had warned him of the unrest and strange vibrations surrounding them. He was glad to know the meaning of the discord. Alfonso's belief in the supernatural had been instrumental in his acceptance of the new information, and it was a relief to have everything out in the open.

Carefully placing the firearm in a secure area, Nate shrugged out of his lab coat, and headed across the room to check the temperature gage on the industrial-size biological incubator. Nearby, two computers crunched out new data based on calculations he'd fed in earlier. The programs would run for hours. Might as well shut down for the night. He turned out the lights, locked up the lab, and headed for a chair in the eating-nook by the kitchen. Alfonso transferred the food from tray to table, and sat across from him.

"You like her a lot, amigo?"

Nate ignored the question and lifted one corner of the ham sandwich, checking out the layers.

"It's just the way you like it," Alfonso promised. "Mayo on one side and mustard on the other. Answer the question, por favor."

"Yes. I like her. Maybe too much."

"How can you like someone too much?"

"You know my track record. When you love too hard, then it's too hard when they leave."

"And when you don't love at all, life is still hard, and you don't even have the satisfaction of having tried."

Nate took a bite of sandwich and washed it down with a swallow of Alfonso's famous after-five coffee. The dash of cinnamon and cream nicely offset the burst of rum. "When did you become such a philosopher?"

"Never mind when I became so smart. Your Uncle Zeb always taught you to listen to your elders. Bliss is obviously something special."

"And worth the risk, I reckon."

Who was he kidding? Head over heels best described his dilemma. He was in the shutes, ready to go. No turning back now. "I guess sometimes falling in love is like bull riding. It can be the most exciting, foolhardy eight seconds of your life. And even knowing you could get busted up but good, you can't resist taking your turn."

"Now you're talking. I won't tell her you compared

her to riding a bull." his friend added, and chuckled. "How is her hermana?"

"A little better, but still struggling to maintain."

The data they'd sent him from the backstreet lab experiments hadn't proved helpful at all. The calculations were very basic and fraught with errors.

"It's a double challenge working with an exotic virus, and the exotic life form it's affecting."

"You will figure it out. I have faith in you."

Well that made one of them. He had never worked so diligently and painstakingly hard on anything in his life, and yet he hadn't solved the mystery, hadn't come up with a cure. Which is one reason he'd put it aside to create the new weaponry for Bliss. Working on the mundane invention allowed him to keep his hands busy while the theories and formulas whirling around in his brain had a chance to percolate.

"I need to go soaring." Only after the words were out did he realize he'd spoken aloud. Fatigue had him more punch drunk than Alfonso's special brew.

"Not at night. No way. And not after a mug of my coffee."

"First thing in the morning," he said, around a yawn.

"What if Senorita Bliss comes by?"

"We can leave her a note on the door as to where we are."

"Si. That will work. Now finish up and go to bed."

****

The warm glow on the horizon whispered the sun was on its way, and the hawks lazily circling overhead suggested the thermals were strong.

While Alfonso poured fuel in the gas driven winch,

Nate uncovered and readied the glider. Exhaustion coupled with the rum had provided the sleep of the dead, and he almost didn't hear the alarm go off. But getting up early seemed a small price to pay to soar through the air like a bird. Something he supposed Bliss took for granted.

On his walk-around inspection, he stopped to check the water ballast. The glider had been sitting for several weeks, but the levels appeared correct, as did everything else. Taping a new yaw string to the canopy, he patted it for luck. Attached in front of the pilot, this primitive piece of equipment indicated slip and skid while in flight, especially important during a turn. After securing the cable to the belly, he gave Alfonso the thumbs up, climbed into the cockpit, and eased the highly polished Plexiglas canopy into place.

The faraway roar of an engine reached him as the winch growled into life, and the glider edged forward, faster and faster, the ground now a blur, his speed rapidly increasing. He had liftoff. When the altimeter hit 900 feet he grabbed the yellow lever on the cockpit panel and released the cable. Gaining more altitude, he soared over Alfonso and the winch and took to the sky.

He relaxed back into the familiar seat, enjoying the challenge and symmetry of balancing the forces of gravity, lift, drag, and thrust. With any luck, as the day warmed and the thermals grew, he could stay up here for hours.

The land below, his land, resembled a patchwork of tall trees, lush pastures, craggy hills, and fresh water ponds. A veritable kingdom. And thanks to the forethought and hard labor of his ancestors, the stewardship of his domain came as a pleasure and not a burden. But the wonder, the fun, the beauty would have been nicer if shared with someone special. This of course prompted thoughts of Bliss. If he could, he'd give her the world. But then she already had the world, this one, and many others.

Still she didn't seem interested in "stuff", but rather she like him—him—not what he owned or could do for her. Nice to be wanted for his brain and not his bank account. Being wanted for his body wasn't too shabby either.

Recalling what they'd shared and how much he'd wanted her the other night, put certain parts of his body in a tailspin, and if he didn't pay attention, the plane might follow suit. Banking right, he caught an updraft, and went ridge-soaring directly into the sun. Eyes squinted against the glare, he felt the craft jostle as if hitting turbulence. The plane yawed to the left. No longer blinded by the sun, he opened his eyes wide, and hooted with laughter.

She'd appeared out of nowhere. Wearing a white peasant blouse, and tight blue jeans tucked into red cowboy boots, Bliss sat straddling the nose of his glider. Like a kid on a ride at the county fair, she waved and laughed. Her small silver wings appeared to move just enough to secure her position, keeping her weight partially suspended, and her presence not altering his payload. The air blasting though her long red hair sent it streaming out around her, giving the illusion of an angel gone devilishly sexy. The next instant, she leaped sideways out of view. He shot desperate glances in a 360 arch. Maybe she'd been an apparition. Then he heard a scratching noise overhead. Leaning back, he drank in the sight of her spread-eagled over him.

She taunted him with come-hither looks, her white peasant blouse askew, exposing one shoulder, the mounds of her scantily covered breast pressed against the invisible barrier separating them. He loved her long lean body, had committed every inch to his didactic memory. The curves, the hollows, the special places capable of setting her pulse to leaping and her breath to quickening.

She made a funny face, kissed two fingers and pressed them against the opaque chaperone. No human duenna could be more cruel than the Plexiglas canopy stifling his need to touch and caress. He checked the air speed indicator, and bet his heart galloped even faster. Catching a thermal, he took them higher, his desire to make love to her climbing right alongside the plane. Would she be okay? He shouldn't be afraid for her safety, after all she could fly on her own, but they were sailing along at over one hundred miles per hour. Guess it was just one more thing he needed to accept on faith. But how could he not want to protect his little warrior woman?

Keeping his head tipped back to watch her, he became dizzy, or perhaps the phenomenon stemmed from the relocation of the blood in his brain to a much lower part of his anatomy. Being this turned on at ten-thousand feet equaled one hell of a rush, but before long, the desire to land and follow through with the urges building in his belly, outweighed the fun of flying.

There were two landing strips on his property, and he headed for the second one. Surrounding the narrow strip of mowed grass, the tall pines and aspen offered cool seclusion. A cabin and shed stood nearby. Another larger building for accommodating the glider and trailer hunkered down on the left. After jettisoning the water, he lowered and locked the undercarriage, checked and stowed all loose articles in the cabin, and with flaps adjusted, went in for a landing.

The glider dipped then bobbed as Bliss rocketed off to one side. The wheels touched down, and he had the canopy open before the glider rolled to a stop. Scrambling over the side he stood beside the sailplane and glanced around. Where had she gone? A pair of boots by the cabin door gave her away. As if removed in haste, one stood upright, one lay on its side. What other articles of clothing had she removed?

Not bothering to unbutton his shirt, he yanked it up over his head and strode toward the cabin. At the open door, he toed off his boots beside hers, and made a concerted effort not to appear to overeager.

"Bliss," he called, giving her the courtesy of announcing his approach. "I love flying with you, girl, but I like the thrill of you in my arms even better."

As he crossed the threshold, she fulfilled his wish.

Throwing her naked body against him, she laced her arms around his neck, and he marveled at her beauty and strength—muscles taut as bow strings, yet with softness found in all the right places.

She made little happy noises around the hungry kisses she teased across one cheek to his mouth. The joy-ride in the air had apparently been foreplay, because she sure seemed ready to get down to business. Lips remaining in contact, he walked her backward around her abandoned clothes, past the kitchenette to the tall footboard of the four-poster bed. She lowered her arms, then the zipper on his jeans.

****

The desire sweeping through her body almost scared the pants off of her. Oh, yeah, it *had* scared her pants off. Now Nate stepped out of his. He'd gone commando, leaving nothing to impede her view. So lean muscled, so panther-esque, like the males of the Katman tribe on Felinius 12—but thankfully without the tail, claws, and overabundance of hair. Nate had just the right amount of furriness.

Without shame she rubbed against his thigh, a she-cat to his he-cat. Grazing the fingernails on her left hand across his chest, she used her other to stroke the part of him newly released from captivity. He grabbed the sturdy bedposts, one in each hand, and nudging her head to one side, nibbled little cat bites in a path along her neck. When her knees went weak, she turned around, and held onto the footboard, pushing her bottom back against him.

Hands on her waist, he jerked her closer still.

"You drive me crazy, woman." He skimmed his hands upward along her torso and cupped her breasts. "I want you so badly, I nearly lost it in the glider."

"Even when you shouldn't be, you're on my mind too. I can't wait much longer," she purred, wiggling her bottom, offering incentive she doubted he needed.

"Never let it be said, I kept a lady waiting."

Quick, deep, and with no preamble, he gave her all he had to give.

Like water and granite, they were two elements as different as their respective species, brought together by love and war. And they were as wild as waves crashing on rock, an unbound natural force with no concern for the world other than this driving desire that wouldn't be denied.

The storm grew stronger, the waves higher and more out of control. Senses on the verge of overload, heart pounding, it took her breath away. But what she felt was more than just physical, their spirits were also intertwined, flying free, enjoying a dance of their own.

When he quickened the rhythm, all circuits blew. A spasm of gratified need thundered through her, hot and blinding, flashing like a neon sign, lighting up her world. Hands cinching her waist, Nate groaned out her name and followed—meeting her on the other side.

Releasing the headboard, she turned and fell into his arms. He held her tight as aftershocks trembled through both their bodies.

Chapter Fifteen

"Nate sure felt disappointed when the data we gave him from Lester Martin turned out to be bogus," Bliss said, to Solace. "But those women didn't die for nothing." She studied the row of deceased women on the board. "We learned what not to do. That's important too."

"And we've figured out what Jones circled in the newspaper." Solace picked up Yana's scrap of paper comparing the positioning to the corresponding column on the previous page. "Real estate. Look, it's up in Black Hawk," she added tapping the copy. "Perfect place to keep out of sight and lots of money changing hands at the casinos."

"Lots of money needing a good scrubbing," Bliss agreed.

Solace attached the article to the board. "Now we know where to look for the low-life."

"Jumpin' Jupiter, I feel a road trip coming on."

"That'd be fun," Solace agreed. "But we can't both go with Port still not out of the woods."

"No, of course not. So how do we decide who's going? Coin toss? Paper, scissor, asteroid?"

"It's all yours. Tanner can't go. He won't be available for a while. He's taking more men to Colorado Springs. And I don't want to go without him."

"What happened in Colorado Spring?"

"A lightning strike started a wildfire near Cheyenne Mountain. They called in the aerial firefighters, and as they circled back to pick up more water, the crew in the helicopter spotted unusual activity. Luckily they radioed it in. When the men Tanner already had down there checked it out, they found a large encampment. No life forms present, but the campfire was still warm, and there were a few pieces of military equipment abandoned in haste. Evidently the mountain is still high on their list of objectives. They wouldn't have been successful attacking from that vantage point, but it's a good indicator things are not all quiet on the western front."

"Boy is Port going to be P'd-off. That's her turf, and she's not down there."

"It's T'd-off honey."

"But you spell pissed with a p."

"Oh, sorry thought you were going for ticked-off."

"No." Bliss shook her head. "Ticked won't cover it. She's gonna be pissed."

"We should go tell her. It might snap her back from wherever she is. And when did you start talking so colorfully?" Solace stared at her with hyper vision. "Oh by Mithras. Are you in love? You're wound up tighter than a Raytheon spring. You should be all mellow and relaxed. Aren't the two of you doing it?"

"I'll say we are. We even flew together."

"You did it Fae style?"

"Not exactly. He has a glider, I have wings."

"Maybe you shouldn't tell me more."

"It was innocent. More like Fae-style foreplay and petting. A wonderful prelude to what we did *after* we landed."

"Then why are you so hyper?"

"He makes me…giddy. That's the only word I have for it. Giddy to the point I don't know what I'm saying. Giddy and girly and giggly. I'll be okay," she added at Solace's doubtful expression. "Part of it is over compensation from the empath vitality drain. I'm still sucking up energy from everywhere. I'm surprised plants aren't dying at my feet when I walk by.

"Okay, I get it. Maybe after your Chi balances out, and the two of you have been together for a while, it will wear off a little. Although I have to admit, Tanner can still make my warrior brain go all girly too."

"I don't want it to wear off," she confessed.

"I don't blame you there. Anyway, I guess you and Nate are elected to go."

"Go?"

"To the high country."

"Oh, right. See I forgot what we were even talking about. I need a margarita."

"You need a protein shake and a workout in the gym. And when you go to Black Hawk, take Noodge. He attacked the sofa again and demolished another cushion."

"Poor baby. My fault. He hasn't been out enough lately. With Tanner gone, maybe Nate could take over part of his training or exercising. We'll definitely take him along."

"Promise you'll be careful. Just reconnaissance, no heroics. Scope things out then lay low. With the Labor Day holiday, the town is bound to be a madhouse over the weekend."

"Labor day. They're celebrating having babies?"

"No. Labor, as in work. They're celebrating a day

off from work. Your Dagda training really did cut into your Earth history classes."

"I got hooked on their literature though. I love their stories and legends. Besides, that's why we have you, sis. You're great at all the history stuff."

Solace stepped closer, brow furrowed. "We'll be the furthest apart since we were reunited. It worries me."

"I know. Me too. I doubt we'll be able to connect with so much distance between us. But I'll be with Noodge and Nate, so I'll be fine."

"I believe you, or I wouldn't let you go. I trust both your men to watch your back."

****

Bliss piled two sleeping bags, a cooler, and a small suitcase-on-wheels at the curb in front of their apartment building. Then adjusting the cowboy hat she had permanently commandeered from Solace, she tried to strike a nonchalant pose. No use Nate knowing how excited the mere thought of spending a few days with him made her feel.

"Sit Noodge. Guard. Good boy."

When she'd asked Nate if he wanted to accompany her to Black Hawk, he'd offered to drive. But she'd forgotten to mention Noodge, and now she hoped he'd show up in something with a back seat. She'd never trust Noodge unattended in the bed of a pickup truck. How could anybody in good conscience do that with any animal?

At the sound of an engine, she glanced up the street. Arriving right on time, Nate eased the vehicle to the curb, cut the engine, and got out. As he came around to her side, he patted the car's hood as he might his favorite horse, and his expression told of his pride for the shiny conveyance. Cherry red with pearly white accents, the car's chrome grill and bumper gleamed in the midday sun.

"She's a beauty. Is it new?"

"Heck no, cowgirl. She's a '57, Chevy Bel-Air, 2 door hardtop. Uncle Zeb and I restored it. I only take it out on special occasions."

"Is this occasion special?"

"You're a special occasion," he countered, bending to capture her mouth in a quick playful kiss.

As the decibel level of Noodge's whining grew intolerable, Nate straightened, and greeted the Rapran. "Hi Buddy, you coming with us?"

The tail wagging and harking, a cross between barking and howling, indicated a definite yes.

"I'm sorry. Maybe he shouldn't ride in your snazzy car."

"No problem." Nate opened the car door, angled the front seat forward, and grabbing up a folded woolen blanket, he spread it out over the seat.

"Now we're good," he said. "In you go boy."

As Noodge bounded into the backseat, he knocked her into Nate. She grabbed his shoulders for support she really didn't need. He always smelled so good, like pine trees and the great outdoors, with his own manly scent thrown in for good measure. She wanted to bite his neck.

Noodge turned around a few times, and after plopping down his giant keister, he licked the side window with a tongue nearly the same size.

"So what's with the sleeping bags?" Nate asked.

Steadying her on her feet, he returned the front seat

to its normal position, and reaching inside, he lowered the back window partway for the critter. "Are we going camping?" he added staring down at the mound of baggage and gear.

"Well we're getting a late start on a holiday weekend," she explained, grabbing some of the items to help store them in the trunk. "I thought all the hotels might be booked."

"I think we'll be okay. Not saying I wouldn't love to sleep with you in a meadow with a million stars all around. Gees, you brought a cooler too? I'm sure they have plenty of food up there."

"It's food for Noodge. He eats like a horse."

"Which is redundant as horses eat hay, and he eats meat which you should never feed to a horse."

"Then how about, because he could eat a horse?"

"A disturbing idea," he said, "but admittedly more accurate." Muscling the cooler on board, he slammed the trunk closed.

She eased onto the front seat, and gazed up at him as he leaned on the car door

"You look beautiful, as usual," he said.

"Thank you," she chirped, as he closed her in.

The girly, giddy syndrome reared up full-blown. She curtailed it just short of the giggling phenomenon. Cripes, she'd faced-down enemies in multiple universes, but her heart beat more erratically in the face of his simple compliment. Noodge huffed as if he were laughing at her.

"Oh hush," she ordered.

Nate climbed in on the driver's side and started the engine.

"Do you know how to get there?" she asked.

According to the map she studied last night, it seemed a pretty straight forward route.

"Been there a time or two," he said, the tone of his voice leaving her to wonder if he could be a midnight gambler as well as a cowboy.

They headed out of Boulder on highway 93. The cooler weather had turned the aspen adorning the countryside into a golden feast for the eyes, and in contrast to the bright blue sky, the trees almost seemed to glow. But as they gained elevation, the vibrant patches dwindled, soon overtaken by rocky terrain. The hills changed to walls of stone, and the road grew more twisty, the gold now replaced by the occasional tenacious evergreen.

Bliss enjoyed looking at the mountains. They were magnificent. But being in them was another story. They struck her as dark and furtive, cold and claustrophobic. Possibly a throwback reaction to when some Fae clans lived in hills and burrows, a condition by which her people could not abide. Impelled by this obscure twist in the DNA, she preferred the high plains, where you could see forever.

As they came around a curve, her side of the car fell into shadow. Drawing her jacket closer, she shifted her gaze to the river rushing by on Nate's side of the two-lane road, the sunny side. The drop-off to the water appeared rather deep, and there was no guard rail. But Nate handled the car like he handled his horses, relaxed and in control, and the car seemed to respond in kind. Hugging the curves and running flat out on the straightaways, he pushed the speed limit a little, of course.

Remembering Nate had been out of the loop lately,

she decided to give him an update on how things stood at present. He knew the reason Tanner and Solace hadn't made a bid for the road trip, so nothing to add there. "Dr. Death is in jail without bail," she began.

"That's good news."

"His lawyer is going for manslaughter, but the Boulder D.A. wants first degree, claiming while Martin tried to save the women, he's the one who exposed them with the bio-agent in the first place."

"Even better news," Nate said, and nodded. "What about Jones?"

"According to our pharmacist-gone-bad, Jones came up with the poison idea, which makes him an accessory on all accounts. If we catch him."

"The authorities don't know he's an alien, right?"

"Correct. And we don't want them to, which is why we have to get to him first. Dr. Death tried telling them about the Reps, but it only gained him a psych hold and evaluation."

"He could use that for several reasons."

"I hope we take Jones alive so he can live in a cage the rest of his life too."

"He's a soldier. Here on a mission. He'll probably fight to the death."

"Maybe. But he's been here a while. He's grown accustomed to living like a Hume, with a nice house, nice clothes, a nice car. And he likes the power and status he's garnered. After the debacle with Smith, he didn't just hole up until further orders came in. He started another business, a few in fact, has an army of mercenary Reps at his beck and call. I'm betting survival, not loyalty, will be his strong suit."

"I like the way you think."

Wow, quite the compliment coming from a brainiac, and an opportunity for a little fun. "Oh, I see," she teased. "You're only fascinated with my brain."

"That's just not true," he protested. "I'm definitely fascinated by all your parts." As if taking a quick inventory, his gaze swept her body. With a raised brow and a sexy grin, he returned his attention to the road.

She sure hoped they found a room tonight—one with a really bouncy bed.

****

About an hour later, they turned onto the main street of Black Hawk, and Bliss felt as if she'd taken a step back in time. The town, sitting cozily between pine covered hills, screamed Wild West with brick-front buildings and sun filled narrow walkways.

"Solace would love this place. It doesn't look as if it's changed in one-hundred and twenty years."

"And one-hundred and twenty is just about the current population—if you don't count the hordes of tourists milling about."

The sightseers were everywhere, decked out in big hats and sunglasses, laughing as they jockeyed shopping bags and souvenirs, and handfuls of edible treats. And like bees seeking the best honey, they buzzed about from one casino to the next.

"Why are the sidewalks so narrow and the street so wide?"

"In the old days, the roadways had to accommodate a horse drawn wagon turning around, leaving folks on foot to their own devises."

Fascinated, she leaned forward peering out the front window. Up ahead on her left, stood a Victorian house dripping lacey fretwork, on her right a new building with a flashing neon sign—what a clash of time and cultures. As the brick façade and red sidewalk canopies of *Bullwhackers'* came into view, she couldn't help but wonder what stories lay behind such a colorful name. The town seemed to hum with present day hopes of getting rich, as well as past memories of fortunes won and lost. But whereas old timers pinned their dreams on mining gold, modern day visitors prayed to lady luck at gaming tables.

"We need to locate the property circled in the real estate ad," she said, glancing around. "I wonder if Jones followed through and bought it."

"According to the address, it should be right there," he said, and pointed. "And I believe you can stop wondering. Before it went up for sale, it went by the name of *The Bull Pen*."

The shiny new sign atop the building indicated the place was now called *The Lucky Lizard*.

"Got to give him credit for some big cojunes," Nate added.

Oh barf. Big scaly green cohunes. An image to surely scar her mind for all times. "His ego is literally out of this world," she agreed. "But I doubt he's hanging out at the casino."

"Probably running the show from one of those fancy houses in the surrounding hills. I phoned the local sheriff yesterday, he hasn't seen anyone fitting Jones' human description."

"The sheriff…"

"Don't worry. I didn't mention the Reps or hint at anything off the wall like alien invaders. Even after the incident at the pond, I'm still having a hard time wrapping my mind around the idea. I get the feeling we'll be pretty much on our own up here."

"Being on our own is the best part."

Nate leaned over and whispered a kiss against her cheek.

Noodge made a sound which could only be classified as a sigh of contentment, and at times like this, remembering they were knee-deep in a plot to take over the earth took concentration. Her prior combat duty placed her in war zones with bombs bursting in air, living hard, and sleeping in a tent if her luck held. This downtime comfort made it too easy to get complacent and drop one's guard. Too easy to dwell on Nate's six-pack abs and roaming hands, rather than military packs and hand grenades.

Trying not to aid and abet such wayward intentions, she went back to people watching.

"Shouldn't we stop and find a place to spend the night?" she asked, as they cruised past the *Isle of Capri* and *The Golden Gate*.

"If it's all right with you," Nate said, slowing down. "I thought we'd stay at the *Wild Horse Casino and Lodge*. It's just up ahead, and pretty much in the heart of things."

"Sounds great—if they have a room. And what about Noodge?"

At the mention of his name, the Rapran whined and shoved his face over the seats between the two of them. Bliss hugged Noodge then gently pushed him back so she could see when they entered the underground facility attached to the building they sought. Parking appeared to be at a premium, but Nate solved the problem by boldly commandeering a space marked reserved.

She hoped it wouldn't draw undue attention to them. Noodge licked her ear, and she figured where they parked would probably be the least of their worries. After making sure his collar and leash were secure, she opened the door, got out, and stood back with legs braced as her Rapran shot out from the backseat.

While he peed on the tire, Bliss established a mental connection with him, stressing they were on a mission, and he must obey her. Nate locked the Chevy, tucked the keys in his back pocket, and taking her hand ushered them toward the backdoor entrance. She loved it when he held her hand. Such a simple thing, yet a skin to skin connection that said *she's with me.*

On his best behavior, Noodge pranced beside her like a pampered pedigreed dog, and all heads in the casino turned to watch as if they'd just been awarded best in show. At the check-in counter, Nate patiently waited for the young woman to finish writing a memo. When she glanced up, her face brightened as if she recognized Nate, and she didn't even blink at the fact he escorted a tall redhead, and an alien critter.

"Mr. Calhoun. What a pleasure to see you. Would you like the usual room?"

Holy criminy how often did he come here?

"Yes, if possible."

"The penthouse became available two days ago. It's clean and ready to go."

"Thank you, Denise." He took the keycard she offered, and turned toward Bliss.

"How'd you do that? She didn't even ask about Noodge."

"I own the place."

Chapter Sixteen

Thunder rolled across the heavens, and echoed into forever as Mother Nature stepped into the path of an oncoming meteoroid. She couldn't remember ever having been this angry, at least not in the last five-hundred years.

Inhaling the breath of the universe, she flung wide her arms, turning loose a wall of intergalactic energy. The wave blasted the meteoroid into a million chunks of cosmic debris. When the pieces hit the earth's atmosphere they would become shooting stars—not a bad way for a meteoroid to end. Besides, what better way to vent her fury than on a rock hurtling through a sentient-free zone? Sometimes, being sworn to oversee all creatures born with the capacity to feel, tore at her soul—especially when some of them were implementing conditions which would surely lead to death and destruction. She tried to remain neutral, but when the good of the greater whole was at stake, she had no choice but to take sides

The Reptiles had feelings, but no conscience. It would be their downfall. Of course the true blame lay with the one who incited this invasion. The one who loved watching chaos ensue.

The one who promised the glory and spoils of war to the victors.

At least now she knew for whom to look. The

question being, where to find them?

****

Bliss relaxed beside Nate on the balcony of their penthouse accommodation. Nate, so unassuming with his country charm and woodsy wisdom. He'd fooled her again. And she loved that her superhero didn't flaunt his wealth.

She longed to sprout a pair of lacey wings, like the ones Solace had fashioned a few weeks before while they dressed for the Country Club dance. Golly, that seemed like eons ago. The impractical frilly wings would be just for fun, but who cared? Being earthbound with Nate constituted a fun she enjoyed immensely.

"What a spectacular way to start the evening," he said, turning to face her.

They stood eye to eye, and what she saw in his gaze ratcheted up her heart rate and made her long to be on a holiday planet where she could pick a tranquil venue to while away days on end with him. But she'd been assigned to Earth to do her job, not to fall in love, or even to fall in lust—duty vs booty. She needed to focus her thoughts and energy on the man who tried to kill her sister, and not on the man trying everything he could think of to save Port.

Not an easy task, however, for when she allowed her empath abilities to kick in, the old school chivalrous ideals she detected in Nate overwhelmed her. Values like family honor, and loving with one's whole heart and soul. Traits the Faes' held dear. In Nate's life, there seemed to be few halfway measures. But such thinking left one open for disappointment, and she didn't want to be one of his.

"Yes, it is a spectacular beginning," she admitted.

"And hopefully it will end equally as well."

"Before we go, I have something for you," Nate said.

Uh oh. Now panic rose to the top of her list of feelings. Please, please, don't let it be jewelry, or something else so personal. Being intimate with Nate constituted one thing, being indebted to him something else altogether. Oh, why worry? Maybe it was another framed photo or flowers. That would be sweet. Evidently, he pictured her more as a female than a soldier. Did he even understand or appreciate what she stood for, or know what being a warrior meant to her?

He dug around in the large suitcase he'd had brought up from the car, and unearthing a bulky item, he turned around and held it out to her.

Her eyes widened in wonder, and words evaded her.

"I asked Mother Nature if it would be okay to alter some of your equipment," he explained, extending the weapon even closer. "She not only gave me the go ahead, but sent me some parts."

The side by side barrels of the particle laser were large-bore and elongated. The stock, beefed up in keeping with the proportions, added symmetry and a badass vibe. Then she recalled where he'd said he'd gotten the parts, and she didn't know what astounded her more, the fact he'd made this for her or his casual tone when he mentioned speaking to Mother.

Mother won.

"You called her?"

"Well no. Actually she called me, regarding information pertaining to Port's condition. And we got to talking…"

"You mean like chatting? Like hi, how's your day going?"

"Again, not exactly."

How could he remain so calm regarding speaking directly to Mother? Those random occurrences still made her nervous—as it did Solace—and even Port. It compared to rubbing elbows with the gods.

"She really is nice," he defended. Lowering his arms, he cradled the weapon close.

"Nice? I have never in my entire life heard anyone refer to Mother as nice. Amazing, incredible, magnificent, scary as hell, but nice, no."

"But you only see her as your commander and chief. I see her as a beautiful woman and…"

"Okay, stop right there." What was he saying? Had he been flirting with Mother Nature? Everybody knew Mercury couldn't keep his hands off her. She didn't want to think about this.

"I was a complete gentleman," he assured, as if suspecting she may be a little jealous. "She said she was glad you and I were getting along so swimmingly and flying high."

Bliss' cheeks burned, no doubt a peachy/pink which she hated as it clashed harshly with her red hair.

"Swimmingly—like when we did it in the pond? Or flying high—like on your glider?"

There went any doubt Mother kept an infinitely close watch on them. For some reason when it came to Mother knowing about her sex life, Bliss felt like an adolescent caught with a Fae boy in the backseat of a landblaster, her blouse open and her pants awry. Embarrassment turned to indignant irritation. Well, who cared? She believed in free-love, the world needed love, living beings needed love, on all levels. What she shared with Nate qualified as a deep longing and desire—but a dangerous feeling if it became all consuming.

"Hey," Nate said, breaking in on her thoughts, "she also mentioned making progress finding the person behind this whole nightmare. That's encouraging, right? Come on now," he coaxed. "Look at your new toy. I call it the Calhoun Special, it's a sawed-off laser shotgun."

She pictured him in his lab, working on the weapon, late at night after a full day of trying to find a cure for Port. He'd probably been exhausted, but he'd done it for her. How could a gift be any more extraordinary and personal?

She stepped closer, and he placed the weapon in her hands. It weighed less than she'd expected, yet the balance was true, and it had a handy over-the-shoulder strap. He'd even tooled some western scrollwork on the recharging plate, including a big B—for Bliss she imagined.

"They were working on something like this back home," she said, admiring the workmanship. "But when we were issued the newly perfected particle laser pistols, they said these might take a while longer."

"They were getting close. Mine's better though and already available." He said it matter of fact, not bragging.

"You better patent this. They'll be clamoring for these all over the multiverse."

"It's already in the works."

"Good thinking. Wonderful." He'd proven to be a smart businessman, as well as a scientist, and roughneck cowboy. He amazed her.

"Yep, registered and incorporated, with the rights and future profits signed over to the newly created DFV."

"The DFV?"

"The Disabled Fae Veterans group. Kinda like the DAV, which I totally support. And it also includes a fund for any animals injured in the line of duty, especially Raprans. That way," he added, his expression a bit sad, "no matter where you are, I'll know you and Noodge will be taken care of."

"What a beautiful, generous thing to do. Thank you." She should say more but couldn't find the words. Noodge gave a mellow woof, and cocked his head to one side.

"You're welcome." He gave Noodge a scratch behind the ears. "We should go. We can drop this character off on the way to *The Lucky Lizard*."

"Drop him off where?"

"I set up a facility behind the casino to accommodate patrons who travel with pets. There's even a few stalls for equines. Sometimes I come up here with one of my horses. It's a great starting point for trail riding."

Again his connection with and compassion for animals stirred her soul. She hadn't thought to meet a male Hume so brave of spirit, yet so tender of heart. He understood the need for freedom in animals and humans and hopefully in Faes. He didn't seem the kind to hold her back or hold her down. If they had to separate, would he be able to let her go? Would she be able to leave?

Maybe she'd been wrong, maybe love wasn't

free—not real love. Maybe it came at the price of surrendering one's heart, but surrender in any form couldn't be found in her Dagda warrior vocabulary.

****

They entered *The Lucky Lizard*, and the wall of noise bombarded Bliss' super-sensitive Fae ears. Unrecognizable music banged along in the background accompanied by the squeals of happiness and yelps of disappointment as patrons took turns winning and losing.

Venturing forward, she studied the customers and employees. Since the Reps were so good at masking their stench and true form, solid detective work and intuition would have to be relied upon to track down any leads.

As agreed, she and Nate headed to opposite sides of the room. Dropping in her money, she played a few slots so as not to stand out too much, and for the first time she wished for bad luck. She didn't need sirens blaring and winner's lights flashing highlighting her position. Glancing around, she decided the dealer at the Blackjack table appeared familiar.

She pawed through her new, even larger, tote and retrieved her handheld, smiling as her fingers skimmed across the laser shotgun. When the list of local Reps in human form popped up on the screen, this guy held the number two position, right behind Jones. They had been together almost from the beginning, and this fellow appeared a little worse for wear. He would have started out on the original transformation serum. Too bad they'd discovered the side effect so quickly, or this one might have been dead by now.

A patron at the Blackjack table, apparently having

had one too many free drinks, turned belligerent. Those around him scattered. The dealer growled at him, his form momentarily shuddering as if the desire to transform simmered just below the surface. A bouncer showed up in the nick of time, and after speaking to the quarrelsome man, he escorted him to the front door.

As players drifted back to the table, the dealer handed his position off to another employee. Bliss followed the identified Rep as he exited the room and made his way down a dimly lit hallway. Using a key, he opened a door then proceeded inside to an office. After running his fingers around the inside of his collar, as if it were too tight, he grabbed up the phone and dialed.

"Yeah, it's me. No, no trouble. Just reporting in as usual. One obnoxious drunk. Pretty good considering it's a holiday weekend. Want me to send you up a meal from the *Cattlemen's Steakhouse*? Okay, you got it boss."

When he made a second call, ordering what sounded like Jones' meal, she memorized the delivery address. It wouldn't be too far away if the restaurant accommodated delivery there.

After hanging up the phone, the Rep strolled over to a small cupboard, opened the beveled glass door, and plucked out a bottle of scotch and one glass. Filling the tumbler half-full, he smacked his lips and savored the liquor. When the boss is away, the hired help will play. She marked him as another Rep who seemed to be adjusting well to the perks of his human form. Whoever thought they were in charge of this invasion might have a big surprise waiting when they finally decided to make an appearance. These Reps had probably never lived so well. And although fighting exemplified their nature, goals could change.

The big lug stashed the scotch, and apparently not a Germaphobe, he tugged his shirt loose at the waist and used a portion of it to wipe the glass dry. With a hearty belch, he stowed the glass beside the bottle. She eased back between the stacks of supplies as he headed in her direction. Drawing the door shut behind him on the way out, he never looked back.

Exhaling the breath she'd been holding, Bliss edged forward and jiggled the knob on the office door. Locked tight. No chance to explore. But she had the address where the food would be delivered. It would have to be enough. About to turn, she heard footsteps at her back. Was he coming back? Reaching to draw a weapon, she braced for the attack.

"Hold up, Buttercup. It's just me."

At Nate's voice, her muscles relaxed.

"I got worried when you disappeared." He draped an arm across her shoulders.

"Did you find out anything?" she asked.

He shook his head.

"Well, I did."

They left via the back door, as she relayed the information about the food delivery.

"Have you heard of this restaurant?"

"Sure, it's just up the street."

They picked up Noodge, bundled him into the backseat of the Chevy, and parked across from the *Cattleman's Steakhouse*.

"What if somebody else placed an order to be delivered?" She drummed her fingers on the armrest.

"They're not known for takeout. I think it would be unusual."

"There," she said, and pointed.

A young man, juggling a large amount of to-go containers, exited a side door, and made his way to a car parked in the employee only area.

Nate started the engine. "Gotta be him. Or an employee done with his shift and taking a very large amount of leftovers home. Do we stay or follow?"

"I think we better follow."

Noodge whined and sniffed the air as if he could smell the food.

"You can't be serious," she joked. "You just had a bag of cat kibble, and two steaks we brought from home."

A humph and a sigh came as a response, followed by a literal tongue lashing of her left ear.

"Ugh," Nate said, slowing down so as not to get too close to the car they followed. "Remind me not to nibble on your ear tonight."

"No problem. Your nibbling can be put to good use in more interesting places." Just the thought set her to clenching her thighs together.

"Are there any girl Raprans?"

The question took her by surprise. She thought a moment, logic dictated they existed, but she couldn't recall ever seeing one. "I guess so, why?"

"You should get one for Noodge."

She noticed he said she should get one, not we should get one. Offers to share responsibility for rearing yet another colossal beastie wouldn't be coming from his direction. "Again, why?"

"Then he'd have someone of his own species to play with."

"We play nice together," she pointed out, "and we

aren't the same species."

"You got me there," Nate agreed, keeping his eyes on the road. "Of course, since we scientists like to be redundantly thorough, I'm going to need more data regarding your playing nice hypothesis."

"Mother told us to give our partners full co-operation.

****

The delivery car turned onto a dirt road labeled *Coyote Run*. Nate drove on to the next lane where he turned around, backtracked, and pulling off to the side, cut the lights and engine. Less than fifteen minutes later the car from the restaurant reappeared and headed back out.

They drove closer.

"I can see lights up there," she said, peering through the window. "We should go the rest of the way on foot."

"Sounds good," Nate agreed.

Although supposedly a recon mission, after exiting the car, they geared up for battle. Bliss holstered and strapped her particle laser around her waist. Then she grabbed her new shotgun for just in case. Nate matched her, decked out in conventional Earth weapons. Noodge gave his "there's Reps nearby" whine, and they headed uphill through the trees and rocks.

"Once we make sure it's him," Bliss said, "we should call for backup."

"Then you'd better start praying now for a decent signal. It can be dicey here in the mountains."

The log house up ahead loomed grandly in the moonlight. But unlike Nate's log home, this one projected an unfriendly fortress-like demeanor, warning visitors off, instead of welcoming them in. They crept around the cement retaining wall bracing up this side of the hilly landscaping, then circled the entire house to get a feel for the rest of the land, and to check for available exits and entrances.

The east side of the house, fitted with floor-to-ceiling windows, overlooked the twinkling lights of the town below. Beyond the glass, a fire burned in the hearth, and the ceiling fan turned lazily overhead. All seemed right with the world. Everything except the fact Jones stood at the foot of the sprawling staircase, suitcases stacked at his feet. Shifting her gaze, she watched one of his goons in Rep mode drag a trunk toward the pile.

"It's Jones all right," Bliss confirmed. "Criminy Dutch. Looks like he's going to make like a lizard and slither out of here."

"You better try to reach Solace and Tanner," Nate suggested.

To her surprise, she got through on Tanner's private number, but only reached a recorded message. Remaining in Colorado Springs, he wouldn't be of help anytime soon. She'd already tried Solace, and even though she was closer, Bliss couldn't connect to her at all, not even to leave a message. This had her concerned. She couldn't feel either of her sisters, not one tiny bit.

"I think we're on our own," she relayed, trying to shake the sense of worry surrounding her.

With their backs to the cement wall, Bliss and Nate slid to the ground to discuss options. As she stared up at the endless night sky, a cluster of shooting stars blazed across the heavens.

Chapter Seventeen

Taking refuge in the dim light of Port's hospital room, Solace stared out the window.

"Oh wow, Port, I wish you could see this meteor shower." She spoke over her shoulder, keeping her back to the room.

Sometimes she couldn't bear to watch Port lying there hooked to tubes and machines. Port the rebel, Port the one always up for a good battle. She fought hard now, too.

"Mother said the poison destroyed not only the cells of your body, it also attacked your core spirit."

Maybe that explained the expression of madness on the faces of the women rescued at the beet factory—and the look on the ones who died in those experiments. Fortunately, the Fae had a stronger psyche than Humes, and the bio-meds suggested by Nate to boost Port's immune system were keeping the damage contained.

Huffing out a big breath of frustration, she paced about, stopping periodically to re-check her handheld. It seemed dead, but it shouldn't be. She'd charged it last night. Passing the window, the fiery display in the night sky again snagged and held her attention. They sure were a long way from home. Feeling a tad homesick, thoughts of going back for a visit crossed her mind. But what about Tanner? She smiled, wondering how she might wrangle permission for him to come with her—

then her Fae senses went on alert. Someone had entered the room.

Spinning around, she threw one hand up in front of her face to block the blinding light. With the other she drew her weapon. The room glowed with the brightness of the meteorites she'd been watching. What the frick? Had they sent someone new to try and kill Port? Why hadn't the guard at the door stopped the intruder?

She crouched into a combat stance—uncertain of what she faced, or where she should fire. Her particle laser suddenly felt too heavy, and exhaustion bore down on her until she could barely keep her eyes open. She should be frightened, but a faraway voice told her everything would be okay—and she believed it.

Someone took the weapon from her hand and eased her languid body into an overstuffed chair.

"Sleep now. I'll take care of her."

She felt rather than heard the words. Felt them and obeyed.

****

"Pretty little Portence. How you hated when I called you that. Of course, that's why I did it. But you were pretty and my being nearly seven feet tall, most beings seem little to me, even all six feet of you."

Reeling-in the light waves cascading from his form, he stepped closer to the bed—holding back the urge to touch her face.

"You're more beautiful now than ever—even with your skin as pale as your hair, and all this infernal equipment weighing you down as it tries to save your life." He visually scanned her motionless form from head to toe, seeing more than flesh and bone. Her body continued to heal, however the life spark flickered, fighting to stay alive. The energy infusions from Bliss had helped, but not enough. Portence needed magic.

She'd dreamt about him. He'd felt it. Felt her terror and hate, just as surely as he'd been overwhelmed by sadness and remorse. She embodied the most cherished moments of his life, and the most regrettable. In his troubled heart he knew she would never forgive him—a penance well-earned he supposed, although she had never let him explain. Regardless, he owed her, and nevermind the risk, he intended to start paying up tonight.

As he lowered the side-rail, energy bled from his fingertips into the metal frame, enveloping the bed in a blur of golden light. What he determined to do, even a sorcerer could only achieve with great difficulty and even greater peril. And if he were found out, it could mean his life. At least this way there would be one good and honorable thing listed in his accomplishments.

He glanced toward the door. Like Solace, the guard outside slept, leaving no worries about being interrupted. The sleep-zone he'd created on the entire floor would hold until he commanded it be released. And the force-field he'd wrapped around the hospital acted as a second level of security blocking all cell phone and satellite connections. They were safe but time came at a premium. His absence would eventually be noticed, his alleged loyalty questioned.

As of late, he cared less and less about such concerns. A future without Portence seemed a more unbearable fate than anything else he could imagine. He missed her to the depths of his being, and had accepted this assignment for the sole purpose of being near her. But twisted by another's dark needs and desires, his noble intentions had become a sordid tangle. And now the only woman he'd ever loved had been hurt.

He reached for and held her hands. They were cold and stiff, and felt half-dead which is exactly what they were. His ever growing anger flared, but forcing personal need and emotion aside, he focused on the here and now. Hopefully, there would be time later to release the pent up fury he harbored. And although he couldn't change the past, perhaps he could bend the future.

Eyes closed, he hummed a sacred note. The sound filled the room until the walls shook, and the windows rattled. Shouting out the rituals in his mind, he called to Port's ancestors. Would she interpret the disturbing of her departed kin as another sin against him? Another transgression to fuel her hate. Considering how she already felt about him it hardly seem to matter. At least this way he knew the life-energy he called upon would be pure, with no harm coming to her, and with no payback expected or bargains to be fulfilled for its use.

Those in the spirit world were usually willing to help—if they heard those in need calling. Most humans had lost the ability to reach beyond the veil, and sadly they didn't care. The Fae believed and often times summoned those beyond for moral support or mental comfort. But asking for physical assistance took a lifetime of learning.

Concentrating harder, his body grew larger. The image he maintained while on earth wavered and filled the room. It went beyond the brick and mortar of the hospital to touch the stars. The ones he called upon came forth, glowing bright blue, like the color of the lifeblood flowing through Portence's veins. He gave thanks then absorbed the life giving substance they offered, his body jolting as they joined with him. He felt the beating of one thousand hearts, the love of family, and pride of ancestry—feelings to which he could lay no personal claim.

Filled to bursting, he gave thanks again, and tearing himself away, snapped back to Port's bedside.

He loosed her hands, peeled the tape from her face, and carefully removed the breathing apparatus they'd forced down her throat. When she gasped, he captured her parted lips with his, breathing the blue vitality of her bloodline into her lungs. She moaned, her limbs vibrating. Lost in a vortex, the heat rushed from his body to hers. Having nothing left to give, he stepped back and calmed the atmosphere. A bit of color highlighted her cheeks. She would be okay.

He touched two fingers to her chest, just over her heart. Now she would also carry the sign of the sorcerer. Another thing to piss her off.

"When you awaken, my love, you will be renewed. Pity you won't remember the kiss I now place upon your brow."

He bent low, pressing his lips to her forehead. He wanted more, so much more, even the mere possibility of rebuilding a bridge he had sadly burned long ago. Finally forcing himself from her side, he left the room, his heart wishing him to glance back, his brain refusing to be tortured even one more second by gazing upon the female he could never have.

He thundered down the hall, robes flying out behind him like a wake of untamed emotion. Waving one hand in the air, he freed the hospital floor from sleep. Groans and muffled voices asking *What happened? Who was that?* echoed behind him.

Reaching the main level, he released the hospital from security mode. He would have preferred keeping it in place, helping to ensure her safety, but maintaining the spell came at too high a price and required his nearby presence.

Gaining the parking lot, he smelled the Reps before he saw them. Regardless of what medications they took to disguise their diabolical form and evil odor, his nose would not be deceived. Had they been sent to take another shot at killing Port? Walking resolutely toward them, he couldn't be happier. They were the perfect targets for the burning need and anger roiling in his belly.

With obvious intentions of forcing him to step aside, the two thugs in human form never altered their course. But when they drew near enough to discern his clothing, they hesitated. Too late now, boys. He pointed a finger at the one on the left, sending him staggering sideways. Drawing a gnarled willow wand from inside his cloak, he zapped the other one with a fatal blast containing all the misery, anger, and desperate longing to be loved eating at his soul. As body-parts flew in several directions, the decimated tissue morphed into Reptile, spewing green blood across the hood of a nearby SUV. The vehicle's alarm activated, sending screams of rage into the black sky—matching the silent screams torn from his heart.

His second enemy, now in scaly-green-eat-your-face-off form, snarled and roared as if in challenge, yet he nimbly moved back and forth, keeping just out of range. Or so the nasty creature thought. This was really too easy.

The Rep roared again, this time as if to bolster his own courage. The sound echoed off the buildings reminding him of the dragons back home. He liked dragons, with their dry sense of humor and ancient wisdom. Except for their leathery hides, these Reptiles were as far removed from dragons as two living entities could be. He would never hurt a dragon, but he could hardly wait to eliminate this odious Rep.

Pretending to be afraid, he shrank back, hoping to draw his opponent closer. The ploy worked. Jaws snapping, clawed hands extended and ready to tear him apart, his enemy advanced. Facing down the beast, he blew across his open palm, creating a blast of wind sending the creature into the air. "Ice you be now, poor wretch." When the flailing Rep hit the ground he shattered into a thousand pieces of pretty green rock.

As he faded into the dark of night, his hate for the Reptiles wavered slightly. Like most beings, they were only doing what they were bred for. Only bowing to someone else's command.

Good intentions notwithstanding, we all have regrets, and we all are to blame.

****

On the mountainside, Bliss and Nate relocated, taking up position off to one side of the retaining wall.

She had a clear view of Jones as he stood calmly before the windows. Hands clasped behind his back, he appeared to be contemplating the world and his place in it—which would be none if she had any say in the matter.

As she watched, thoughts of Port jolted through her mind. The vision, unbidden, lacked the usual feeling of sorrow and concern. In fact, the sensation felt uplifting.

This energy didn't originate from her sister. Regardless of where it came from, she glommed onto the feeling, taking it as a positive sign, even one of hope.

Nudging her with his elbow, Nate broke her train of thought and the feeling slipped away. "Guess it's up to us to alter the saurian son-of-gun's travel plans," he said.

"You got that right, science-boy."

Her lips twitched at his use of the rare technical reference for lizards—their private joke. But before they could take action, Noodge came to attention, hackles up, a low malevolent growl shaking his body. The cause became evident as a Rep in full regalia materialized out of the woods. He halted, stared directly at them, and let loose with a gruesome bellow of a laugh.

"How the heck did they know we were here?" she muttered.

Glancing around, she spotted a security camera in a fir tree, but by the Rep's cavalier attitude, she doubted he'd spotted Noodge.

"At the ready," she whispered, to the eager Rapran. "We need to see if he came alone, or if he has company for you to play with."

The drunk beast cavorted about, his weapon in one hand, a bottle of what had to be hard liquor in the other. "Slay the Fae. Slay the Fae." He stopped leaping around long enough to send a spate of bullets their way from what sounded like an AK47. "Love to eat them faeries, and nibble on they wings."

"I don't think so bozo. Have at him, sweetie."

As Noodge bounded forward, she and Nate fired, giving him cover. The Rep stopped laughing, and before he could defend himself, Noodge bowled him over backwards. His weapon sailed through the air, landing several feet away.

Knowing the Rapran was in his glory, and could take care of himself, Bliss fired her spiffy new laser shotgun at the wall of windows. The glass shattered like hydra-ice sending a shower of sparkling particles into the brightly lit room. Hot damn, she'd have to be sure and thank Nate properly for the new weapon. Through the broken wooden window frames, she watched Jones fleeing to another room, leaving his luggage behind.

"He's gonna run," Nate warned.

Figuring he'd use the back entrance, they sprinted around to the other side of the mega-house. Over the sound of her labored breathing, she heard the grumble of an engine starting. The pitch sounded too high for a car, and not growly enough for a motorcycle. As they rounded the corner, Jones came straight at them on an ATV. Nate leaped to the left, she took the right. They hit the ground, and rolled, firing after the fading taillights.

Jones escaped beyond the cleared area surrounding the house. But the next layer of terrain resembled the surface of an asteroid riddled planet. Tougher to negotiate, the angle nearly straight up, it offered him no choice but to slow his pace.

"He's heading west," Nate pointed out, as they dodged trees and scrambled up the face of the ridge behind him.

The laser shotgun slung across her shoulder bounced reassuringly against her back as she clawed her way along at Nate's side. Being accustomed to great heights, the 9,000 foot elevation had little effect on her.

and even though it took its toll on Nate with heavier breathing, he didn't slow down, leaving her to admire his stamina and fortitude.

"If I remember correctly," she said, "the only things up ahead are a few abandoned mines, and several very old cemeteries."

"Maybe we can make him a permanent resident."

"I like that idea. Think I'll take to the air, and try to head him off."

Just about to conjure wings, she heard the engine sputtered and quit. She remained still, straining to listen, willing her heartrate to slow.

"Out of gas?" she queried, as Nate stepped to her side

"Or the carburetor isn't set for this altitude. Either way, a boon for us."

Ditching the idea of taking flight, she stayed earthbound, and as they crept closer, her pointy ears now fully extended picked up the Rep's cursing and the sound of dry vegetation crackling.

"He's taking off on foot. Still heading west."

"I'm right behind you," Nate said, as they followed their enemy.

Having superior sight, Bliss led the way, and with the moon nearly full she didn't bother to activate her heat finding powers. But when Jones passed through the iron gate of the cemetery she halted dead in her tracks. Nate crashed into her from behind, and not in a good way.

She couldn't maintain battle-mode, and also keep her psychic guard up. And if she entered the ancient land of the dead unprotected, the spirits would overwhelm her.

"I can't go in there on foot."

Apparently recognizing the anger and frustration in her voice, and trusting she knew best, he didn't question why. She shoved the shotgun into his hands, shed her jacket, and conjured a set of combat wings. Edged in silver, they gleamed in the moonlight, leaving trails of light as she gently flapped them.

"I'll take air-recon," she said, reaching for and retrieving the shotgun he still held. "We can't let him get away."

Before she could take off, Nate grabbed her by the arms. "Remind me later to tell you how sexy you look with your red hair wild and free, and your cheeks flushed with battle courage." He swooped in, gave her a serious kiss, and then headed out on foot.

Airborne, with no one to see, she indulged in a quick giddy-girly smile then hovered, taking stock of the situation and the surrounding area.

Noodge howled in the distance. The sound of victory. A new set of yips told her he was heading in their direction. *Good boy*, she mentally praised. She wouldn't feel so bad leaving Nate alone on the ground if Noodge fought at his side.

Gliding silently overhead, she spotted Jones weaving his way in and out of the obelisks and wrought iron fences, and with weapon in hand she took aim then hesitated. From this distance the shot pattern would be wide, and Nate headed for her target too, closing fast. She wouldn't forgive herself if he were wounded by friendly-fire. Trading shotgun for pistol, and a more precise shot, she dove down between the trees, straight at her enemy.

Pain ricocheted from shoulder to spine as her left

wing hung-up on a low-slung telephone wire. Focused on Jones, she never saw it coming. Her body twisted in midair, leaving her with only one thought, *don't lose your weapons*. Doing a three-sixty, and with no time to regain control, she gritted her teeth, and crashed to the ground.

Gasping for a decent breath, she groaned and sat up. Gees, that hurt. She hadn't airdropped since she was three years old. The hardest part of learning to fly had always been the ground, and on that score, nothing had changed. After a quick assessment, she declared herself okay—physically. Psychically she needed to get the heck out of here.

Spirits from the acres of centuries old burial plots rushed at her. Some were solicitous, some angry, some confused. All combined it felt as if she were being battered and torn by ethereal hands. She knew they weren't really there anymore. They were gone on to the afterlife, but the paths for some had been hard won, with no one to pray for them, and for others the suffering had been great. This ground sorely needed to be re-consecrated, if indeed it ever had been.

Seeming to recognize her distress, Jones circled around, morphing into Rep mode on the run. Nate altered course coming at her from the other side. She couldn't think clearly, felt weighed down by the mournful energy of the dead and bereaved. Hands over her ears didn't help, the sounds bombarding her felt as if they came at her from the inside out.

Fighting the pain, clawing at the dirt, her fingers curled around the stock of the shotgun. She rolled onto her back, and stared up into Jones' evil face.

He smacked his lips. "Nothing like a late night Fae

snack."

Bliss fired point-blank sending him staggering back, saving her butt, but not killing his. Protected by his thick hide, he recovered and gained his balance, closing in fast. How these monsters could move so quickly still surprised her—and might be her undoing.

As he tensed to leap on her, a blur of fur sailed over her pronated body hitting Jones in the gut. This time he went down for the count, and his screams of anger and pain mingled with the lost souls still howling in the wind and streaking across the tombstones.

Nate hauled her to her feet and dragged her toward the perimeter of the cemetery. Stumbling and scrambling along as best she could, Bliss eighty-sixed her wings, and collapsed to the ground just beyond the rusted gate. Nate knelt at her side, one hand on her shoulder as they both momentarily shifted their gazes in the direction of growls and roars.

"You okay?" Nate asked, now studying her. "You're shaking. You must be cold." He shed his wool jacket and wrapped it around her.

"Thank you. I'm good—now. How about you?"

"Hardly had any fun at all. Things were just getting interesting when Noodge horned in."

"He's in the zone. I wouldn't try to intercede."

"Hadn't planned on it," he agreed. "Guess he turned out to be all the backup we needed."

"We make a good team, the three of us. I love…working with you."

When Nate hesitated to respond, she felt more afraid then when she faced Jones in full Rep mode. Couldn't he at least say he loved working with her too? True, she hadn't offered him forever-love, but couldn't he be her for-now-love. It was just as real, just as important, just as painful if unrequited.

****

Didn't Bliss love him more than just working with him? He believed she did, had to trust that she did, because he was a goner. At this point he didn't even care if she broke off a piece of his damaged heart and fried it with her particle laser. He admired her courage. Adored her eternal innocence wrapped in gritty sensuality. If need be, he'd risk all for a chance at what could be.

Taking a deep breath, he tried to formulate a reference for the way he felt. But love was beyond science, and beyond reason, leaving him the comfort of neither. Or perhaps being shot at is what gave his life this new and sudden sense of urgency. He needed something to blame for what he was about to say.

"We're the best team west of the Mississippi. But I don't just love working with you, Bliss, my wonderful, out-of-this-world, highflying, straight shooting, math challenged little Fae Warrior. I'm in love with you all the time, around the clock."

She appeared stunned, then about to speak. Not sure he wanted to hear her response, in case it wasn't what he hoped for, he gained his feet. "Noodge probably doesn't need help, but I'd better go check on him."

Knowing she couldn't follow, he jogged toward the graveyard, giving himself time to get it together.

Chapter Eighteen

Bliss sighed in contentment and studied her two sisters through the steam rising off the hot tub. Port's miraculous recovery, and the take-down of Jones, had happened only two days ago but right this minute it seemed eons had passed.

"I can't believe we're all together again," she said.

Port remained silent, eyes closed, head tilted back on the built-in pillow.

"Me neither," Solace agreed, reaching for a plastic glass shaped like a big red chili pepper. It contained their favorite drink—high test margarita.

At least all three of them usually preferred the bite of salt and tang of lime. Tonight, Port sipped on water with lemon, a good idea considering what she'd been through. Her physical health, although near perfect, remained fragile, and her mental state seemed dark and troubled. Not meaning to pry, Bliss clicked off her empath abilities. If Port wanted to talk about what might be troubling her, it had to be her decision.

"Here's to Jones being dead and Port being alive. Alive and well." Bliss held her glass out for a toast.

"It's been so boring with no one to boss us around," Solace agreed, tapping plastic on plastic. "And hopefully this is the beginning of the end for the Fae-eating invaders."

"It's only the end of the beginning," Port said,

green eyes now open and flashing, her expression scary serious. "And the next part is really going to suck,"

"Why would you think such a thing?" Bliss asked, lowering her glass.

"If the worst wasn't yet to come," Port snarled, "*he* wouldn't be Earth-side." She grazed one hand across Eolh, her new tattoo. The rune sign marked the gentle swell of her left breast, sitting there as if holding its breath just above the waterline.

"But it's the sign of protection," Bliss pointed out.

"A coiled snake would better represent him. And I don't want or need his protection."

Bliss knew the entity who had cured her sister in her hospital room was also responsible for the horror she'd felt in Port while transferring white energy into her to help keep her live.

"The nurses on your floor remember the incident as a visit from some kind of a modern day Archangel," Solace noted.

"They think what he wants them to think. He's the devil's homeboy"

"But he saved your life," Bliss reminded, then shrank back from the searing anger emanating from Port's eyes.

"He also left me to die once. And the part of me he destroyed will never be brought back to life. I'll never love again with my whole heart. And know this—he's as mercenary as ever. Don't mistake what he did for me to mean he's on our side in this battle. Leopards don't change their spots."

"The leopards of Camorae do," Bliss said softly, trying to abate the hate with a little humor. Dark energy would be detrimental to Port's recovery.

She glanced at Solace for support. Her dark-haired sister wore the *yikes change the subject* expression, as she splashed around to break the deafening silence. Noodge whined as if he too felt the discord.

"We were so worried about you, Port. We love you, and we're so glad you're back. I don't care who's responsible."

Port bit back a response. Bliss guessed for now, it would be best to drop the subject. Besides, the mood of comradery in the hot tub had gone under. "I'll get dressed and take the critter out for his last walk of the night," she offered.

Sky-clad, she climbed out of the hot tub, gasping at the shock of cold. The temperature on the balcony registered much colder in the evenings now. Snagging one of the robes off the nearby lounge chair she wrapped the soft terrycloth and her arms around herself trying to get warm.

"Freaking brrrr." Teeth chattering, she could hardly speak. "Reminds me of Epsilon-b. Were you guys assigned there too? I don't know how the Norse-guard tolerates living there on a permanent basis. Six weeks was enough for me."

"Me too," both Port and Solace said, in sync. They each gave a shiver, despite the warmth of the hot water. This shared memory brought a whisper of happiness to Ports face. "I'm for bed," she said, rising. "Thank you again guys for taking such good care of me."

Bliss tossed her a robe as she gave up the hot tub.

"We'll soon be playing ducks and drakes," Port added with a full-fledged laugh at their expression, her humor momentarily restored. "I know. Isn't it the weirdest saying ever? I had a darling of a night nurse who loved the phrase. Even in my fugue state, I heard her say it each evening when she tucked me in. Turns out she's British, and a huge fan of old literature. Apparently it means everything will be okay."

"It's an expression from the Regency era," Bliss said, her enthusiasm for Earth literature finally coming in handy. "I love it. The Sisters of Anu will soon be playing ducks and drakes."

"Aw, now look what you started." Solace rolled her eyes in mock irritation. "Bliss hasn't mentioned The Sisters of Anu for weeks."

Each time anyone said Anu, Noodge howled as if to honor their ancestors.

"A…nu, A…nu," they chanted just to incite him. He raced back and forth the length of the balcony, nose in the air, baying like a hound. Bliss laughed so hard she hiccoughed, and for a moment it felt like old times, like when they were young, or like when they had first gotten back together.

Lately, they'd been wrapped up in a mix of tangled emotions. Somehow she and Solace felt responsible for the Reps getting the better of them and making Port ill. Survivor's guilt perhaps. Why Port and not one of them. And Port seemed in a tizzy because her past had bled into their present with possible detrimental effects to the future. But things would be better now, they'd cleared the air somewhat, and unless it was by choice, nothing would ever again separate the Sisters of Anu.

"On that note, or I should say earsplitting howl, I bid you goodnight." With a little wave, Port headed for bed.

"Goodnight, Port," Bliss acknowledged.

"Yes, goodnight, Port." Solace stretched out in the

empty tub and floated to the top. "I think I'll soak a while longer. I'm waiting for Tanner to call."

Of the three of them, Solace enjoyed the hot tub the most. Bliss loved the water too, but sometimes the heat drained rather than renewed her. A brisk walk with Noodge sounded energizing though.

"Okay. Come on Noodge. I'll change clothes, then we'll head out."

****

Port locked the sliding glass door leading from her bedroom to the balcony then drew the drapes tightly shut. With her back to the wall, she gave a bitter laugh at the vain attempt at security. If he wanted to, Malachi could enter any room, no matter how protected.

If only he hadn't come back. She'd been trying so hard to forget the past and appreciate what she had. And she certainly needed to stop obsessing over what she'd lost. Easier said than done, of course. Again she grazed her fingers across the new tattoo. It felt hot to the touch. When this Earth invasion was put down, and the Fae Warriors were no longer needed, she would request a leave to visit a glam planet and have it removed.

Suppressing the desire to scratch and tear the symbol from her body, she lowered her hand to her side, and crawled naked beneath the covers.

Eyes closed, she willed herself to sleep. They'd soon be playing ducks and drakes. She muttered the phrase like a sacred mantra—if only it could be true.

****

The next morning, the three sisters along with Tanner and Nate, sat around the table at the Green Goddess office. The Mother board blipped and transformed as Mother, on speaker phone, added new information.

"You've done a brilliant job eradicating the Reptiles from your sector."

The praise in Mother's voice comforted Bliss, however past experience told her a big BUT may be coming.

"Smith, Jones, and White were in the upper echelons of the Reptile organization. Eliminating them has crippled their effort here in Boulder. We believe NOAA and the National Institute of Standards and Technology are off their immediate list of targets. Nate, anything to add?"

He nodded, and verified the information. "To ensure the clocks remain safe, the NIST is on permanent lockdown. And I'm on permanent loan to the Army E.T. Squad. If you want me."

"Of course we want you," Bliss wholeheartedly defended.

"He means militarily," Solace gibed.

"Focus children," Mother put in. "Our efforts in Colorado are now shifting to the Cheyenne Mountain facility. You've been down there recently, Tanner. What are your thoughts on the situation so far?"

"Working in tandem with the MSG, Military Support Group, we've disrupted two take-over attempts. First they went with the *new hire* angle just like at NOAA, trying to get an operative on the inside."

He hesitated for a moment and Bliss suspected he thought of his little buddy Ralphie, killed and tossed from an airplane when Jones was in charge of murder and mayhem.

"We intercepted their agent," he continued, "who is

now being detained in Colorado Springs. In their second attempt, no doubt inspired by the previous lightning strike, they set brush fires ringing the facility. An ineffectual and clearly desperate attempt to breech the most impenetrable command center on Earth. Which is not to say we didn't take the attempt seriously.

"While NORAD and other defense operations have been moved to Peterson Airforce Base, the mountain is still an integral part of the North American Aerospace Defense Command. It's the last bastion."

"If the Reps are intent on destroying and taking over the general population, why would they even be interested in access to the mountain?" Port asked.

"Good question," Tanner acknowledged. "The Reptiles are infiltrating globally. If they can coerce or takeover a foreign government, they can use the facility as a global command center. If the other countries hold out, they can use it as a safe house. It's totally self-contained. Even has underground potable water. We think whoever is behind the invasion will want the mountain to belong to them."

"You're correct in that analysis," Mother concurred. "And what this means, is that everyone will be relocating today. You three ladies will continue to work with the Army E.T. squad which Tanner oversees, and I'd like to have Dr. Calhoun onboard as a civilian consultant. We appreciate the help you've given us so far, and can use your scientific knowledge down there as well. You can set up your own red team."

Bliss breathed a huge inner sigh of relief. She wouldn't be separated from Nate. At least not yet. "We're taking Noodge, right?" The thought of being separated from him also tugged at her heart.

"Yes," Mother reassured. "I'm quite pleased with his performance so far. And it's obvious he's formed a bond with all of you. It would be cruel to take him away right now. I'll also facilitate setting up your information board once we know where you'll be housed."

"If I may, ma'am," Nate all but interrupted Mother, reminding Bliss of his special connection to their generally intimidating leader. "I have a place in the Springs I think could accommodate all of us. And as the terrain there about is pretty rugged, I'd be glad to bring down a string of horses for our use."

"Excellent, Mr. Calhoun. Extremely generous of you. I knew I could count on you." A lilting tone softened the edge of her voice dwindling almost to a purr. Wide-eyed, the three sisters glanced at one another. Tanner gave a snort of laughter, and Nate grinned and sat up straighter, totally acting the teacher's pet.

"Travel safe. Mother out."

Bliss gave Nate's shoulder a punch. "Mother's got a thing for you."

"I'm sure it's the hat," he defended, reaching for and settling the Stetson onto his head. "The romance of the West, etcetera, etcetera."

"Well, if we're through analyzing Mother's voyeuristic interests," Tanner said, gaining his feet, "we better hat up for real and head to our new base of operations. We'll be on the down-low until we meet up again. Leave the LARS you were using," he said to Solace. "We've got Mk-19's in the action zone."

Solace jumped up and threw her arms around his

neck. "By Jupiter, I love it when you talk military."

"What can I say, babe, you bring out the warrior in me." He hugged her back and gave Solace a quick kiss as his hand slid from her waist to her bottom.

"How about," Bliss suggested, "Nate, Noodge, and I bring the horses, and you two and Port convoy or drive down together."

"Sounds good," Tanner agreed at everyone's nod of consent.

Noodge dragged his blanket across the room then went back for the motorcycle tire chew toy which he deposited on top of the rumpled mess. Just how much did the critter understand? Bliss scratched him under the chin. "We won't forget your toys," she promised. "Or you."

Chapter Nineteen

Bliss loved Nate's barn.

From the gentle breeze sending dust motes dancing in shafts of light, to the big tortoiseshell tabby cat stretched out in a puddle of afternoon sun, comfort and peacefulness hung in the air.

Stepping around the laid back feline, she inhaled the fresh scent of this season's baled hay. "You are an amazingly brave cat, Mrs. Maxwell," she called over her shoulder as she gathered bridles and laid them out on a work table. "Even Noodge gave you respect after your first encounter. And I noticed, you in return, give the goose a wide berth, and so it goes. I'm happy you all get along so well."

"Mrs. Maxwell is a smart lady, just like you." Nate returned from the tack room carrying the last of the five saddles they were taking along. He set it beside the others then stood before her in all his cowboy glory. She settled one hand on his chest, the softness of the well-worn chambray shirt belied the well-defined muscles she knew lay beneath.

He studied her face, those diamond blue eyes drinking her in. Looking back, how had she so mistakenly pegged him for a geek, a nerd, a shy brainiac? He'd done it on purpose, that's why. He'd projected an image he believed would keep her at a distance. It hadn't worked. Her fascination for him started the minute she'd laid eyes on his fake geeky self. And being around Nate only amplified her attraction to him—and for him. She was glad now he felt comfortable being his true self around her.

They both took a step forward, and their hips met, zipper to zipper, hot need to hot need. Her wing ports twitched, and she glided one hand down the front of Nate's jeans. They were tight with enthusiasm.

"If we're going to reach Colorado Springs before dark," he warned, his lips only a breath away from hers, "we need to get on the road."

"Right now, the only thing I need to get on is you."

"You never said it back."

"What?" His words took her by surprise.

"You never said you loved me."

Trying to delay her response, she opened the top button on his shirt, leaned forward and kissed the warm expanse of muscled chest. He groaned out a reaction then gripping her upper arms eased her away from his body. Guess he wasn't going to let her off the hook that easily.

"I can't promise you forever love." Might as well be truthful.

"I understand. And believe it or not, I don't care."

"I do love you, Nate. I love you today, right this very moment. And I'll love you for as many days as Fate or Mother or the Supreme Being gives me to share with you. That's all I can promise."

"That's all I can ask."

She'd been afraid to admit any of this to him, but again he'd surprised her, he accepted their situation, and was willing to enjoy to the max what minimum time they might be granted.

Her declaration inspired affection, and not knowing when they might be alone again, they jettisoned their clothes in record time, and toppled onto the drover coats he'd laid out. Bliss ended up on top, straddling his thighs. Mrs. Maxwell leaped onto a bale of hay for a front row seat.

His fascination for her tattoos lived on, and he gently traced their pattern with his fingertips sending shockwaves through her body. Mesmerized, she studied her human—the one man on earth who claimed her heart and her body. How glad she was they'd found one another.

Before she could luxuriate in such a wonderful thought, or enjoy the simple pleasure of being naked— the ultimate freedom, he maneuvered her onto her back. His wicked expression stated he couldn't wait a moment longer to have all of her. Matching his need, she took him in, one slow glorious meeting of two souls.

In such a short time together they'd discovered their special rhythm, and their auras meshed as brilliantly as their bodies. She asked for more, he fulfilled the request, and raking her fingernails down the length of his muscular back, she urged him on. Making love, such a generous gift, could also be a delightfully selfish indulgence, nothing else felt as good. Racing to the finish, not wanting it to be over, yet unable to ignore the need to quench the desire, she gave herself over to the inevitable, and this time they jumped over the rainbow hand in hand.

Still connected in body and mind, they clung together, gasping for air, sharing the last of the dwindling heat and the intermittent tectonic trembling they couldn't control.

As if to say "nice performance", Mrs. Maxwell leaped to the ground, padded over, and flopped down beside them, contented and purring.

****

Starting out on their trek late worked to their advantage. Traffic on I-25 had thinned, and they tooled along at a fast pace. Or at the fastest pace you'd want to drive a seven ton, big as a bus, loaded with five horses, vehicle.

Soon the houses and other signs of civilization thinned out along with the cars. The immediate terrain, rugged, dry, and rocky, held onto hope in the form of greenish sagebrush. Farther west, the rolling hills gave way to distant snowcapped mountains.

When they hit Monument Hill, crosswinds buffeted the top-of-the-line horse transport, but Nate took it all in stride, remaining cool and calm. Relinquishing control had never come easy for Bliss, nor did putting her trust in someone else's abilities. This phenomenon held true on or off the battlefield. But Nate's self-confidant, yet easygoing style, had her giving it a good try.

"How long have you owned the property down in Colorado Springs?" she asked, wanting to get a feel for where they were heading.

"Again, thanks to Uncle Zeb's belief in geographic diversification, it's been in the family for years. Considered worthless scrub back in the day, now it's prime real estate, which I intend to keep as undeveloped as possible."

Nate could make millions selling-off land for shopping malls and housing developments, but he seemed happier preserving nature—another thing she liked about him, and maybe why Mother found him endearing. Please let Mother's interest be an innocent passing fancy. How could anyone compete with a goddess?

She slid her gaze sideways and studied him. He caught her looking—her cowboy/physicist hybrid—turned Indiana Jones.

"What?" he asked.

"You're enjoying the adventure. Even the mayhem, and near death experiences."

"Yep, I sure am, partner. Didn't realize how boring my life had become until you came along."

"So you've traded bored to death, for jousting with death."

"No. I've traded wasting my time looking back, for enjoying the here and now."

"Then I'm doubly glad I'm here, in-the-now."

"Me too."

She remained silent, but the song in her heart seemed so loud you'd think he'd be able to hear the words. Giving herself permission to be stupid happy, she purred on the inside, just like Mrs. Maxwell who rode with the horses.

After Nate had declared his love for her, she feared everything would change, but most things remained the same. One constant would never waver, they were two soldiers—and a Rapran—on a mission, heading for if not all out war, at least a giant friggin' skirmish. She had no say in the matter. After this, she could be deployed somewhere he couldn't follow. Oh what dreary thoughts. She refused to let them beat into silence the melody skipping through her mind.

"Thank you again for the laser shotgun," she said, steering the conversation back to a happy subject. "Every girl should have one."

"You're welcome, again. They've upped the ante haven't they?" he asked, out of the blue.

"Yes. No more pseudo-nice guys in suits, or small bands of murdering thugs with personal agendas. We're way beyond dealing with simple mafia privateers like Abbott and Costello."

"Frank Costello," he said not missing a beat, and politely not pointing out her mistake, "crime boss of the Luciano family."

"Yeah, that's it. They'll probably go all military on us. And with discipline and a firm hand eliminating dissension in the ranks, they'll be formidable. As far as brainpower, you could out think all of them put together. Smith and Jones were rare examples as far as being complex and long range planners. Reptiles are doers, not thinkers."

"So we're back to needing to know who's calling the shots."

"It would help. Mother has a lead but for some reason she's being elusive, which makes me both curious and nervous."

What if the entity behind all this really was the being that saved Port? Right or wrong, she would forever be grateful to the creature for giving her sister back to them. She couldn't dismiss such an important fact, couldn't get it out of her mind, which compromised her objectivity.

Life seemed to be getting complicated on every level. When the Sisters of Anu had reunited, it had been such a rush, all for one and one for all. They were together night and day, fighting side by side, spending all their leisure hours together. Then Tanner had stolen Solace's heart and her time. And now she had Nate. Could their new sister-bond stretch big enough to accommodate their ever expanding lives? There were so many people to love. So many people to lose.

Being a warrior seemed easier when she walked alone. All her time and energy focused on only one thing. But to be honest, she'd followed the path of the warrior by necessity and command, not by choice. And while she was good at and enjoyed being a warrior and serving Mother, didn't she have the right to a satisfying personal life as well. Or even the right to change her mind as far as her career. She hadn't given it much thought until now. If the choice had been hers, what would she have been if not a warrior?

She thought of Noodge curled up in the space behind the seats, and the five beautiful horses and one cat housed even farther back. Using her empath skills to help animals had been her fantasy. The bittersweet taste of dreams-lost made it hard to swallow. Those had been little girl dreams. But one never knew what the future might hold. Turning off such thoughts, she concentrated on the spectacular sunset, pretending Mother had choreographed it just for her as a personal apology for carting her off to military school all those years ago.

"You're being awfully quiet," Nate said, slowing the vehicle.

"Just thinking." She lightly rested a hand on his knee, a symbol of closeness not a sexual invitation.

"One of my favorite sports." He gave her hand a pat, in a totally platonic manner. It felt good.

As their speed decreased, she scanned the area, but

couldn't see a turnoff or lane. Probably still up ahead a ways. You didn't make sudden stops and quick turns in this ginormous vehicle. They edged to the right and took what appeared to be a rarely used exit, which turned into a dirt road. Even at a crawl, the headlight beams jumped and heaved in counter-rhythm to the ruts over which they bounced and shimmied.

"Hadn't planned on being out this way again until next spring, or I'd have asked the country to give the roads a good grating."

"You mean you didn't anticipate being conscripted into a then nonexistent Army E.T. squad to fight reptile creatures from another world. I'm shocked."

"I sure as hell didn't. At least you were part of the deal." He put the transport into a lower gear as they turned off the main road and headed up a small hill. "Finding you came as the biggest surprise of my life." His expression turned serious, maybe because of the dicey driving conditions, or maybe because he didn't know if the surprise was good or bad.

Before she could ask, they dropped down into a valley, and all she could think of was *I wish I could call this place home.* A small lake sparkled off to the left making her twitch with fond memories of their previous water activities. Foothills obscured The Front Range, and offered a backdrop to the log home, red barn, and artistically scattered out-buildings. Fenced fields lined the much smoother private dirt drive, and the pastures showed flecks of green beneath the tall dried grass toppled sideways by wind and rain.

"You didn't bale these fields."

"Nope, left it for the deer and the antelope. It's been a dry season, they'll winter hard."

They headed for two sturdy uprights, and a hand-hewn sign hanging from the crosspiece.

"Why Compass Rose," she asked, repeating the words burned in the wood. Being a devotee of old maps and space charts, the name intrigued her.

"Of all Uncle Zeb's holdings, I like this one best. It's a good place to clear the mind and find direction. I come here when I feel I've lost my way, so in essence it's my compass rose. Smaller than the place outside Boulder though."

"Smaller, but I think more cozy."

"Good." When they reached the uprights, he eased the vehicle to a stop. "Passenger does the gate," he added, giving her a nudge toward the door.

"Okay. It'll feel good to stretch. Can I let Noodge loose?"

"Sure. But we'll have to secure him in the house when we unload the horses."

Having heard his name, when she opened the door, the Rapran vaulted over the seat and planted his feet on the ground before she could do the same. As she swung wide both gate panels, her sweet critter gave his banshee howl and sprinted on ahead, a blur of fur and high spirits. Mentally zoning in on him, she issued a stern warning to stay within mind-shot then she stood by to close-up after Nate drove through.

He eased forward a short distance, stopped, and lowered the window on her side of the vehicle. "Hop in. We can leave them open."

She touched base with Noodge one more time then climbed aboard.

"Tanner shouldn't be too far behind us, and Alfonso will be up later," Nate explained. "He hates driving the highway, so he's taking the backroads, bringing up food for us and hay for the horses. There're a few bales from last year in the barn, but we'll need more if we plan to stay long."

"You're lucky to have each other."

"Yes, we are. I owe him a lot, although he wouldn't see it that way. He calls you my muy bonita señorita. And he thinks you're good for me."

"What do you think?"

"I think he might be right."

"I'm glad he accepted what my sisters and I are, and why we're here."

"Alfonso believes in many unusual philosophies. It runs in his family. And he was clever enough to already know something was afoot."

Nate jockeyed the vehicle parallel to the barn, cut the engine, and clicked what resembled a garage door opener. The huge sliding barn door panels parted, and lights came on inside a building larger than some homes they'd passed on the way. Wooden stalls capped with metal edges lined each side of the rubber-matted cement walkway. Here and there, wrought iron benches and metal feed bins broke the line of sight.

She got out of the vehicle and met him at the back, where he handed her a set of keys. "For the front door of the house," he said unlatching and opening the rear of the transport. She nodded, and went to round up Noodge.

Settling the Rapran in the house with fresh water and plenty of food, she stepped out onto the porch and watched while Nate worked. The horses unloaded without a hitch, seemingly undisturbed by the ride down. Nate turned on the auto-waterers and gave each animal hay, his movements sure with no wasted effort as if he'd done it all a thousand times before. Such tasks and rustic chores had probably been performed on this land for hundreds of years. It spoke of tradition and simplicity and living free. What would it be like to come home to this every night?

Solace and Port would never be content here for long. Just like when they were young, they needed adventure and travel, and were forever fantasizing about leaving. Whereas she'd enjoyed growing up on the commune, and hadn't really wanted to leave. She felt homesick, yet wished to stay here. How's that for a conundrum? Her emotions were as scrambled as eggs.

Life seemed more complicated since she'd fallen in love. There, she'd admitted it to herself. She truly loved Nate. Her heart fluttered, and she couldn't catch her breath. Emotion overwhelmed her, and she felt…scared. Scared and weighed down, as if she'd hit double gravity. Unzipping her jacket, she tore free of it, and threw it on the ground. She didn't know why, but she needed to be airborne. After hours sitting in the truck, and with her emotions in a tizzy, she needed the freedom of flying, as well as some high atmosphere air to clear her mind.

Thoughts of home and her ancestors had her sprouting wings of sacred willow. In the Golden times, before Mankind declared himself ruler of the Earth, the Fae and the Elements had an infinitely closer kinship. Wings of willow were special, less maneuverable and harder to maintain, but when you glided at just the right angle, the air passing through the openings sounded like the wind singing.

Leaping off the porch into the night sky, she sought

the inky darkness.

****

When Nate reached the house, he ran up the steps, nearly tripping on Bliss' abandoned outerwear. He picked it up, and glanced around. Stunned, he caught sight of her in the sky. Holding the jacket close, he inhaled her scent. He wished he could be up there with her, but maybe she needed time alone. He could understand that need. They had both been through a lot lately and at hyper speed.

When he'd first come to stay with Uncle Zeb, he'd nursed a fawn back to health. Man, how he wanted to keep her. But just like Bliss, its need to run free was part of what made it special.

Chapter Twenty

One of Nate's three guest cabins worked out perfectly for their temporary HQ, and they held their first meeting there the next morning.

Bliss reached for a bagel then passed the basket of breakfast goodies to Solace and Port. Tanner had been up for hours, and had already demolished one of Alfonso's special he-man breakfasts back at the main house. Nate still worked there on outfitting a temporary lab with the equipment Alfonso brought down last night. She'd catch him up later regarding their briefing.

Dressed in combat boots, camo pants, and a black tee, Tanner paced back and forth in front of the Special Ops board. The Mother board, set up next to his, allowed the sisters to coordinate and compare information. With his favorite Jericho 941 pistol holstered on his hip, Tanner appeared ready for or rather appeared to be hoping for action.

Port's partner had scheduled a meeting with her for tomorrow. A military man and a surgeon, he'd shown an extraordinary aptitude and interest in alien medicine. So much so, Mother decided to put him through a rigorous training course in Fae biology, anatomy, and physiology. As far as Bliss knew, he would be one of the few military doctors on the planet able to perform surgery on Fae Warriors.

Unfortunately, the prospect of finally meeting him

seemed to garner little enthusiasm from her sister—not even a show of disdain. Port continued to train with them, but she remained closed off, all business rather than her normal playful sarcastic self.

"According to Mother," Tanner began, "the Reps are working on a new subterranean E.M.P. system."

"Electromagnetic pulsing seems rather futile," Port said, at least showing interest in battle preparations. "Are they really hoping to penetrate Cheyenne Mountain with its 25-ton blast doors? The infrastructure is designed to deflect a nuclear detonation."

"If nothing else, it shows creativity," Tanner countered. "It could also be false chatter to throw us off. They're becoming less scattered and more military in their thinking and technology. Either way, from now on, we'll be frequency hopping when we're communicating out in the field. No use letting them in on our plans.

"They're gathering someplace, but so far we haven't found their camp. They're lying low. I have a feeling Jones was the last Rep living overtly in human form. And thanks to Bliss and Nate, he's no longer a problem."

"Don't forget Noodge," Bliss put in, wanting to be sure her baby got due credit.

"And thanks to Noodge," Tanner agreed, glancing over at the critter where he lay as if guarding the door. "In reptile form, the enemy is able to rough it, and live off the land pretty much undetected in the surrounding foothills."

"How about a fly-by with thermal imaging," Solace suggested.

"Again, in their cold blooded reptile form, if their

surroundings are cold, they'd hardly make a blip on the equipment. And it's possible they aren't even in this immediate area which means we'd be wasting time looking for them."

"More soldiers on our team would be helpful," Port said. "How are we doing on new recruits for the E.T. Squad?"

"For obvious reasons it's slow going. And we're inferring E. T. stands for Extended Training rather than Extra Terrestrial. Less chance of causing undue panic from those who don't pass muster. One of our major hurdles is keeping this war subverted and not engaging the general public."

"How about the new weapon Nate's working on?" Bliss couldn't help but be proud of him. "It sounds promising."

"There's one geek I wouldn't mind watching my back," Tanner admitted. "Nate's been a great asset to the team. Unlike regular EMP equipment, this deterrent uses millimeter-wave electromagnetic energy to stop and turn back an advancing adversary.

"A beam of waves heats the enemy's skin causing severe pain and making the adversary flee the scene. Theoretically it should work on Reps just as well as any other species. And unlike explosives, it's quiet and less likely to cause collateral damage."

"But it isn't lethal." Port sounded disappointed.

"No. But it's good to have it in our arsenal, and if somehow captured or copied it can't hurt civilians. That's all I have. Anybody else want to add anything?"

The room remained silent.

"Okay then," Solace said, gaining her feet. "Let's meet on the training field at oh-nine-hundred, your choice of weapons."

Bliss checked her watch. Until the appointed time, she decided to find a peaceful place to do a little meditating.

Port stretched and headed toward the door. "I think I'll track down Nate or Alfonso, and see about riding one of the horses."

"You want company?" Bliss glanced over at Solace. Neither one liked the idea of Port going off on her own. They weren't exactly in a war zone, but they were darn close.

"No, I'll be okay."

****

Ever since Malachi had come to her, Portence felt as if she prepared for two battles—the obvious one and a new one, all about him. Maybe after she partnered up with her Hume, it would take her mind off her worries, forcing her to focus on what she'd come here for in the first place.

How weird, everyone seemed to have somebody special in their lives. Everybody but her. Mother'd done a good job of pairing her sisters with Humes seemingly made to order. Each pair possessed a special connectivity. Still a waste of time where she was concerned. No Humes, that was her rule. Go Fae or stay away.

Malachi was half Fae. Half Fae—half sorcerer—and all bad, as far as she was concerned.

He had to be somehow tied to this invasion. Or had their prior association led him to find her in the dream-world as she fought for her life? She let out a growl, startling the chickens now fleeing from her path, as she stomped her way across the yard to the barn. Why had he waited so long to come to her?

Using the walk-through door, she entered, and ambled along the line of stalls. The horse Nate had assigned her, a beautiful dappled gray gelding, poked his head out when she drew near. She stopped in front of him, and he nickered and nosed her shoulder as if he knew they were meant to be a team.

She gave him a scratch behind one ear, and tugged on his forelock. Ever since being poisoned, her long white hair sported bluish/gray streaks, not totally unattractive albeit a bit odd. The hue blended well with her horse's ethereal smoke colored mane.

"He likes you."

She turned toward the unexpected voice. Alfonso set his shovel aside and stepped forward.

"Mouse doesn't cotton to everyone."

"Cripes, Alfonso, you gave me a scare."

"I apologize, senorita. I see you are thinking thoughts far away."

"You do, huh."

"The barn is a good place for such endeavors. You would like to go for a ride?"

"I planned on it, but maybe I'll just brush Mouse. How'd he get a name like that anyway?"

"When he was born, he was sickly, and seemed so small and the color of a mouse. Now, he is strong and large for his breed. And very beautiful."

"So why didn't you give him a new name when he grew up?"

"It is good to remember the battles we fight and overcome. It makes us stronger and helps us to believe anything is possible."

Port nodded and kept brushing.

"Of the five horses we brought down, he is the lonely one. Like you."

That was kind of spooky. His statement sure hit home. "Don't tell me you can talk to horses."

"Something like that," he admitted. "They called my grandma bruja. It skips a generation so I guess some of it landed on me. They also say good things come to those who wait, but I think you are the kind who seeks out and fights to the death for what they want."

"Damn straight," she said, feeling better already.

****

They spent a good portion of the day in combat training, stopping only once for lunch, another Alfonso special featuring green salad, fresh fruit, hamburgers for the meat-eaters, and avocado, cream cheese, and tomato sandwiches for the weed-eaters. They were hard pressed to go back to drilling after that, but Tanner accepted no excuses.

Solace volunteered to test the capabilities of the now famous laser shotgun. Port tore a bale of hay to pieces with repeated bullseyes of her atlatl. In the hands of her sister, this primitive spear became as deadly a weapon as any modern day armament. But Bliss stuck with hand to hand, practicing her skills on a mixed martial arts target.

By evening, they were spent, but happy. Warfare often represented hours of training, even hours of boredom, punctuated by moments of terrifying deadly combat. To wind down, they all went to the barn to do evening chores. The main events being shoveling and feeding, with silence reigning as if everyone were lost in their own thoughts.

Finally, they gathered around the dinner table.

Tanner's men were bivouacked in the forest creating a perimeter guard, and Alfonso sent another deliciously prepared meal out to them. Those in the ranch house supped on the same, with the addition of his after-dinner-high-test coffee thrown in for good measure.

Sleepy now, Bliss wandered the bedroom she shared with Nate. Where had he gotten to? Other than dinner, it seemed she'd barely seen him all day, and she missed him.

Glancing at the books in the floor to ceiling shelving, she discovered an impressive collection of science fiction, including well-worn copies of *A Princess of Mars, The Gods of Mars, and The Warlords of Mars*, by Edgar Rice Burroughs. She couldn't help but smile as an image formed in her mind of a tousle-haired boy intently reading one of those books, stopping only to glance up in wonder at the night sky. Nate really did love the mystique and adventure offered by the multiverse. Maybe someday she could take him out there to the great beyond. There were portals to accommodate humans—ones needing special permission, not easily obtained.

Grabbing a thick cozy sweater, she tugged it on over her head, and stepped out onto the second floor balcony. Not a cloud in the sky, the air as crisp as the apple she'd picked right off the tree at lunch. Her wingports twitched, but she ignored them. Although he'd never said anything, she knew when they'd first arrived and she'd taken off without warning, Nate had been concerned. Arms folded, she leaned against the rail.

A movement to her right caught her attention, and her mouth dropped opened in surprise, as a remarkable contraption rose up and halted in front of her. Her cowboy had gone steampunk. She never knew what to expect from Nate. A quality she very much enjoyed and admired.

By normal standards the hot air balloon dimensions were very small, and the heat source surprisingly quiet. A box suspended under the balloon-opening glowed unusually bright, emitting waves of heat which traveled upward to keep it inflated. Resembling a small canoe, the elongated basket sported two small tail fans, their pleasant whirring sound barely discernable.

"Welcome, to my latest endeavor," he greeted, with a flourish and a bow.

The literary classic *Peter Pan* came to mind when Noodge popped up beside him. Captivated, she grasped the hand Nate extended, and scrambling over the log railing, took a leap of faith landing in his waiting arms.

Sitting side by side by side in their blanket-lined nest, he snugged her close, and stared up at the sky, his eyes full of wonder like the boy she'd been picturing. Noodge's eyes were wide too, as if flying wasn't his favorite sport.

"It's so quiet. How did you do this?"

"Mother really appreciated the idea of the DFV, and knowing I like to play with Otherwordly stuff, she gave me a heat crystal."

There he went again, praising Mother.

"We could use this as an observation craft," he pointed out, "or our enchanted hideaway."

"I quite like your second idea best."

Reaching over, he tugged on a rope. The knot unraveled, and the ends slipped through his fingers setting them free. "I know how much you enjoy flying, so I thought this way we could kind of share the experience."

His thoughtfulness brought tears to her eyes.

As their heavenly cocoon rose beyond the rooftop and then the trees, Noodge settled down, leaning up against Bliss. He even peered over the edge, giving a startled woof when a bird flew by. Nate sat on her other side, fiddling with the heat crystal, taking them higher and higher. Soon only stars stirred above them, matching the stars she had a feeling were shining in her eyes. She couldn't be happier drifting along warm and snuggly between the two males who made her world so special.

Her Fae ears detected a phone ringing somewhere down below. Who could it possibly be? They were all together here—except for Mother. That thought threatened to quash her sweet fantasy. But throwing caution to the breeze carrying them along, she refused to be distracted. The days ahead would offer plenty of time for warring and worrying and obeying the rules.

Tonight was for being together and sharing the magic.

Fae Warriors Glossary of Terms and Places:

Atlatl: Used to increase the leverage in throwing a spear. It is the first compound weapon.

Anime: Japanese Adventure Cartoons.

Aqueous II: A training planet, mostly water.

Camorae: A planet in the Redshift 7 galaxy. Chameleon DNA, mixed with other animals allows them to change color at will.

Caronium: Planet where the purest gold in the multiverse is mined.

Carpathena: Planet of the yogi masters.

Ceti 9" Home of the Manshees.

Cronos 12: Where the male Fae Warriors are fighting Outworlders.

Crystal Cosmos No. 5: Solace's favorite perfume.

Crystalline B: The ice planet where crystals are mined in the frost fields.

Darrius III: Planet of the salt fields.

Darrius V: Trash planet of the Crap-eater Megaderms.

Epsilon-b: Planet of ice caves.

Exosphere: The outermost region of the earth's atmosphere.

Kepler 186f: the Fae Warriors' home planet

Light-years: The distance light travels in one year. (Nearly 6 trillion miles).

Mercury: Mother's messenger "boy" and lover.

Metrosexual: Metropolitan heterosexual.

Milesians: The ancestors of the modern Irish.

MMA: Mixed martial arts.

Mystica: The planet of illusion.

Nanosecond: One billionth of a second.

Norse-guard 12: One of fifty fabricated planets ringing

the edge of our universe.

Out-worlders: Those beyond the home galaxy.

Paradise III: A recreational planet.

Parsec: 3.26 light years.

Prion: Imperfect protein, causing conditions such as mad cow disease.

Proxigean Spring tide: An extremely high tide, very unusual.

Rapran: Companion animal, looks half mastiff and half Bengal tiger, with a touch of kangaroo.

Remedium 5: A healing planet.

Rigel 5: The prison planet.

Syzygy tide: When the earth, moon, and sun are aligned.

Saturnalia cream: Made on the home planet for soothing bruises and wounds.

Teraheathan planet: Known for art and spun glass.

The Dragon Lords of Anu: The offspring of the fallen angels (Anunnaki).

The Sisters of Anu: Bliss' super hero name for the three sisters.

Trooping: Fae traveling the woodlands in joyous groups, especially on Equinoxes and Solstices. Tuatha De Danann: The people of the goddess, ancestors to the Fae.

Pigeon Fever (Corynebacterium pseudotuberculosis) is a real disease affecting equine, and other large animals. Just like Nate, I hope someone finds a better way of combating this often deadly condition.

Here's a neak peek at the next book in the series:

Portence

by

Gini Rifkin

Fae Warriors, Book 3

Chapter One

Present day Earth, Colorado Springs, Colorado

Portence Goodeve marched through the underbrush as if leading a military charge.

Hard to believe she was finally going to meet this Lance Lawson guy, her new partner, not that she wanted one—once had been enough. It was the principal of the thing.

She glanced around, her field of vision limited by the thick stand of fir trees she navigated. At least meeting Dr. Lawson on the combat practice field beat the heck out of meeting in a stuffy office, or worse yet a hospital—where she'd spent entirely too much time lately.

Cheyenne Mountain would have been her first choice, of course. Touring that facility, a likely Reptile target, topped her current list of things to do—job-wise. Her personal list started and ended with only one name and one mission.

She shoved a branch out of the way and wondered what the good doctor would be like. The perfect combination of military and medicine, or so she'd been told. Gees, another doctor in the mix, it was starting to feel like a Mensa reunion. Okay, so what if her new partner was a geek? Her sister's geek, Dr. Nate Calhoun, had turned out to be a great guy—for a human. But see, that was the other thing. Her new partner was not only a brainiac, he was also a human. Probably just as well. She'd sworn off humans, or Humes as the Fae usually referred to the species. No possibility of romantic entanglements, and no possibility for a conflict of interest.

But screw all this speculating and contemplating. Action, that's what she wanted and needed. Ever since she left the hospital and got her mojo back, she thought of little else but securing the planet, and tracking down scaly Rep-tards—her new personal word for Reptile bastards. She'd come back stronger, her endurance greater, her muscles redefined. The new improved model of herself—Portence Rebuilt.

She just wanted to *do the job.*

Back in the old days, those three words had gotten her through many an unimaginable situation. It would keep her strong now too.

Raised voices, drifting on the breeze, grabbed her attention. She clicked on her hyper vision, but until she cleared the dense forest, visual confirmation remained impossible. Now the sound of moans and crying overrode the original voices. She quickened her pace. What the heck was going on? Had there been a Rep attack? When she said she wanted action, she hadn't meant right this minute.

Shedding her heavy jacket, she jogged forward. Although the black long-sleeved top she'd worn beneath the jacket helped deflect the branches, she still activated her silver bracelets—changing them into body armor to shield her hands and forearms. Always best to be prepared.

Particle laser at the ready, she picked up the pace,

dodging tree trunks and slapping branches out of the way. Nearly there, almost to the edge of the forest. Activating her wingports, the set of furled battle wings tore through the material of her top like it wasn't there. Another piece of her wardrobe ruined.

As she ran, she grew taller, her ears went pointy, her muscles taut. Clearing the field of trees, she cloaked her image and shot straight up into the air to hover and assess. Injured beings were scattered across the practice field. Blue blood stained the bandages and the ground. Only blue blood—no green or red. Her heart seemed to stop, then trip forward double time. The wounded must be Fae, but how was that possible? Were her sisters, Solace and Bliss, among the casualties? Except for the three of them, there were no members of the Fae Warrior Alpha Team in this sector. *It can't be them. It couldn't be them.* The words screamed through her brain as she dipped in for a closer look.

Those rendering aid appeared to be Earth hospital personnel. Surveying the surrounding area, she searched for the velociraptor-like mercenaries she was itching to take-on and eliminate. Where were the scaly Fae-eating lunk-heads? Not getting a visual, or detecting the gagging smell of wounded Reptile, she hit the ground running and flash-moved to the center of the action. Something wasn't right. She dropped cover, startling several nearby people to their feet, mouths agape.

"Who's in command here," she thundered.

Silence fell over the entire group, and they stopped as if frozen in place. All but one person—a large, broad-shouldered, well-muscled, male Hume. Dressed in hospital scrubs, he strode forward, and with his military haircut, steely-eyed glare, and take charge attitude, he seemed more suited for snuffing out a life rather than saving one.

"Sweet Mother of God," he said, coming to stand before her.

"Not sweet and nobody's mother," she shot back.

Standing tall, wings at attention, she challenged his over six-foot-frame, meeting him nearly eye-to-eye. "What the hell's going on here?"

"You're magnificent," he continued, as if not hearing her words. "Just look at her," he murmured to those now gathered near. "This, my weary colleagues, is why you have been training so hard. Why I have pushed you to the limits." He walked around her, checking her out as if she were an animal on exhibit. It made her want to gnash her teeth. Instead she flapped her wings, and gave a snort of laughter when he had to sidestep out of the way.

The *patients* were up and walking around, bandages and IV tubes dangling, medical equipment abandoned and ignored. They weren't Fae, and they weren't injured. A heads-up on what they were doing here today would have been nice, and would have saved her a near heart attack because she thought Solace and Bliss had been injured. As he came back around full-circle, she jabbed a finger into his rock-hard chest, bringing him up short.

"Hold on there, buddy. Who are you?"

"Forgive me. You must be Portence Goodeve. I'm Dr. Lawson, but please call me Lance."

One starry-eyed female *patient*, standing behind him, sighed and glanced adoringly at him.

Port snapped her battle wings shut and eighty-sixth

them, sending up a cloud of dust. Well wasn't that just dandy. What was Mother thinking? She'd been partnered up with *McStudly*. She'd heard about doctors like him. While she'd been in the Fae clinic, the staff had constantly played the TV in her room, and like it or not, she'd been forced to binge-listen-to reruns of some famous hospital show named after a medical textbook. Using that data as a reference to human behavior, *McStudly* seemed to be the correct nomenclature for this quintessential jock. What an arrogant asswagon.

"Well, Lance, I repeat, what the hell is going on?"

Seeming to finally perceive her anger, he took a step back. "Carry on everyone," he instructed those standing around gawking. "Follow me, Miss Goodeve."

As she did just that, she fought the urge to insist he call her Major Goodeve. Her true rank was a tidbit unknown to her sisters. They'd never let her live it down. Besides, her rise up the promotional ladder had occurred while doing special ops. More secrets to which her sisters were not privy.

He led her to a tent, held the flap aside, and waited for her to enter. Her adrenaline evened out, but the flush of being in combat-mode still warmed her cheeks and blood, making the chilly autumn temperature a welcome relief. A couple of deep breaths helped to calm her thoughts.

She supposed she should be thankful, not pissed off. Lately she had one incredibly short fuse, not a good thing for a civilian or a warrior. These Humes were obviously training hard to learn about caring for Fae in emergency situations—she could at least respect that endeavor.

Slouching down onto the camp chair he offered,

she returned her new partner's stare. If he were waiting for her to get the ball rolling, they could be here all day. At least he was easy on the eyes.

"I knew you were coming, but you still took me by surprise. You're the first Fae I've met and in warrior mode to boot. It was just too much."

"You're telling me you have no practical experience healing my kind."

"Well, we're focused on triage and surgery, we couldn't very well go around doing unnecessary operations just for the fun of it. I know you've been ill, and I'm sorry none of our trauma expertise could be of use. But as we are at war, first-responder techniques and emergency surgery seemed the areas upon which to concentrate."

"Makes sense," she grudgingly agreed. But it also meant they'd be using Fae for practice when one got injured.

"In addition, we'll be assuming the day to day Fae emergency duties, taking the pressure off the U.S. Army E.T. Squad. With more human soldiers in the mix now, when the time comes, the Army will need to see to their own. And my group will see to you...your kind...you guys. That sounded rude somehow."

His initial surprise and excitement seemed to have waned, and his previously wide eyes drooped a bit as he considered her. "We've had over half a century to contemplate, investigate, and cogitate what happened in Roswell, New Mexico, and every other day brings a new science fiction book or movie, but casually accepting the presence of extraterrestrial beings still comes hard."

"Yeah, well humans seem pretty alien to us too."

He took to the chair several feet away, and ran one hand across his face, then down his chin as if to wipe away the fatigue now evident in the slope of his shoulders. He appeared tired, and by the gray all but hidden in the buzz-cut he wore, older than she initially thought.

Grabbing a canteen, he opened it, took a long drink, and then offered it to her. Accepting, she downed a healthy swig and handed it back.

"Being a soldier, and a doctor, and a human, I'm the liaison, or hub in this gloriously twisted amalgam of warfare and healthcare. So if you have any questions, I'm your guy. We're pretty much set up now, but the vetting process for personnel took longer than expected."

She didn't doubt that for a minute.

"And now we're finishing up a helicopter landing pad so injured Fae can be shuttled in from outlying areas."

He said all this with great pride, but without conceit or arrogance, and his humble attitude elevated *McStudly's* status to *McMight Have Possibilities*. For him to be in charge of all this, he had to be at least a lieutenant general.

"Sounds like Mother made a good choice when she picked you for the job," she praised.

He shrugged. "Time will tell."

As the cold set in, an unstoppable shiver cascaded down her spine. Dr. Lawson grabbed a quilted camo jacket, and tossed it to her. It fit well, and felt old school and familiar.

"The portable MRI machine arrived yesterday," he said. "I've never seen one so small. I'm sure it will prove indispensable working in the field."

He continued to expound on various pieces of medical equipment and procedures, but her mind began to wander. As long as he knew how to use this stuff, she really didn't care. She was a soldier, a warrior, no time for anything else. It's what kept her going, and for better or worse, what made her who she was.

For better or worse. Which one had won, or was she a permutation of both? Had Mother Nature done her a favor or a disservice accepting her application to the SCI? For nearly ten years, Space Counter Intelligence had been her all-consuming life. It had been exhilarating, testing her on every level, physically and mentally. It had also broken her on both. But she had healed completely—almost.

The military gave her life structure, kept her busy, leaving little time for wallowing in the past, or wasting time dreaming about the future. The trick would be preventing both from screwing up the present.

During her current assignment, she'd been shot at, almost blown to smithereens, and poisoned near to death—considering the mission, not totally unexpected physical assaults. But now *he* was somewhere on the planet, and her heart and soul were in jeopardy too. The earth might be heading for a Reptile Armageddon, but as far as she was concerned, her old partner Malachi was the biggest threat of all.

A word about the author...

Gini Rifkin writes adventurous romance—past, present, and into the future—sometimes with a bit of magic or fantasy, but always with a happy ending. When not reading or writing, she greatly enjoys caring for a menagerie of abandoned farm animals on her little patch of land in Colorado. Her writing keeps her hungry to learn new things, and she considers family and friends her most treasured of gifts.

Other titles by Gini,
available from The Wild Rose Press, Inc.

The Dragon And The Rose
Lady Gallant
Iron Heart
Special Delivery
Victorian Dream
A Cowboy's Fate
Solace

Thank you for purchasing
this publication of The Wild Rose Press, Inc.

If you enjoyed the story, we would appreciate your
letting others know by leaving a review.

For other wonderful stories,
please visit our on-line bookstore at
www.thewildrosepress.com.

For questions or more information
contact us at
info@thewildrosepress.com.

The Wild Rose Press, Inc.
www.thewildrosepress.com

Stay current with The Wild Rose Press, Inc.

Like us on Facebook

https://www.facebook.com/TheWildRosePress

And Follow us on Twitter
https://twitter.com/WildRosePress

www.ingramcontent.com/pod-product-compliance
Lightning Source LLC
Chambersburg PA
CBHW070341260626
47160CB00003B/1107